Langston stared into Trish's eyes, aware of the feel of his body pressing into hers, aware of his hands still wrapped around her waist, his fingers splayed against the bare flesh of her stomach beneath the loose T-shirt. Aware of her hair, in complete disarray with pine straw jutting from the dark curls.

She stood and brushed herself off. "What are you doing here, Langston?"

"Nice to see you again, too, Trish."

"I'm not sure it's safe for you to be here with me."

Not that he was going anywhere. There was no way he could walk away from her as long as she needed him. But there wasn't a chance he'd let her sneak back into his heart.

Dear Reader,

Having moved to the small town of Montgomery, Texas, two years ago, I have fallen in love with Texas and the cowboy lifestyle. When I decided to write a series set in my new home state, I wanted to capture the spirit of the ranching families with their strong ties to the land. I envisioned the Collingsworths as a family bound by the old traditions, men whose word can always be counted on. But the Collingsworths are also on the cutting edge and have made their mark not only in ranching but also in the oil business. They are a family to be reckoned with and the mysteries facing the heroes and heroines are right out of today's headlines.

Be sure to watch for future stories from the FOUR BROTHERS OF COLTS RUN CROSS mini-series. You're always welcome at Jack's Bluff Ranch, where sexy and brave cowboys are the order of the day and where true heroines will settle for nothing less than true love.

Joanna Wayne

24 Karat Ammunition

JOANNA WAYNE

MILLS & BOON

Pure reading pleasure™

*First published in Great Britain 2009
by Harlequin Mills & Boon Limited,
Eton House, 18-24 Paradise Road, Richmond, Surrey TW9 1SR*

© Jo Ann Vest 2007

ISBN: 978 0 263 87268 2

46-0209

ABOUT THE AUTHOR

Joanna was born and raised in Shreveport, Louisiana, and received her undergraduate and graduate degrees from LSU-Shreveport. She moved to New Orleans in 1984 and found the mix of cultures, music, history, food and sultry Southern classics, along with her love of reading, a natural impetus for beginning her writing career.

Now, dozens of published books later, Joanna has made a name for herself as being on the cutting edge of romantic suspense in both series and single-title novels. She has been on the bestsellers list for romance, and she's won many industry awards. She is a popular speaker for various writing organisations and at local community functions and has taught creative writing at the University of New Orleans Metropolitan College.

She currently resides in a small community forty miles north of Houston, Texas, with her husband. Though she still has many family and emotional ties to Louisiana, she loves living in the Lone Star State. You may write to Joanna at PO Box 265, Montgomery, Texas 77356, USA.

CAST OF CHARACTERS

Trish Cantrell – Terrifying secrets from her past may keep her from having a future.

Langston Collingsworth – President of Collingsworth Oil who is called on to protect Trish.

Gina Cantrell – Trish's teenage daughter.

Matt, Bart and Zach Collingsworth – Langston's brothers.

Jaime and Becky Collingsworth – Langston's sisters.

Lenora Collingsworth – Langston's mother and the new acting CEO of Collingsworth Enterprises.

Selena Hernandez – Trish's best friend and employee at the Cottage Boutique.

Gary Packard – Homicide detective with the Dallas Police Department.

Phil Caruthers – Defence attorney hired to represent Trish.

Aidan Jefferies – Langston's detective friend.

Celeste Breemer – Langston's fiancée.

Carlos Carletti – Wealthy boutique customer who has a shady background.

Prologue

Trish Cantrell rinsed her stemless wineglass and placed it on the top shelf of her dishwasher. She might as well call it a night. It was only ten, but she hadn't slept well since she'd been abducted from a restaurant parking lot at gunpoint last week. Fortunately, her teenage daughter was away, volunteering in a summer camp program for disabled children.

The carjacking had left Trish so shaken she hadn't been able to work for two days. The threatening phone call that followed demanding she return some mystery video had upset her just as much. But that had been a week ago and there had been no more contact. She had to move past this. Carjackings happened in the city. It was the new way of life in America.

She stretched and started back to the bedroom, then went back to double-check the deadbolt on the front door. She seldom went in or out that way, but checking locks had become a habit long before last week's incident. She'd wait and set the alarm when she got back to the bedroom so that it would sound instantly if a window or door to the outside was opened or the motion detector was set off. Another habit that she'd had for years, though it was on her mind more now.

The floor creaked as she walked to her bedroom. She loved the house, which she'd bought almost on her first day in Dallas. It was almost seventy-five years old, but the previous owner had remodeled it without losing any of its original charm. The hardwood floors and the double fireplace that opened to the den and dining room were a couple of its most terrific features. And all of it cost less than the much smaller flat she and her daughter had in London.

Trish stopped to check the door that led from the laundry room to the garage. Locked, as always. She never forgot to stop and do that when she came in. In fact her briefcase, purse and keys were still sitting on top of the small household toolbox where she'd set them in order to turn the heavy double bolts.

A shuffling sound came from the hall, setting her hair on end. She shrugged. It was nothing but the old house settling. Despite the mental reassurance, a chill slithered along her nerve endings. She waited, and there it was again.

And then she saw him.

Adrenaline rushed her bloodstream as the man stepped closer.

"I told you to give up the video, but you just wouldn't listen."

Chapter One

Lenora Collingsworth smoothed her ash-blond locks and noticed the new smattering of gray. At fifty-six, a few gray hairs were to be expected, but that didn't mean she had to like them. She liked the chaos that was contributing to their arrival even less.

She looked down and let her gaze linger on the picture of her late husband, marveling as always that she missed him after all these years. Things would be different if Randolph were still alive. He'd take the reins of control of his family company from his ailing father. The transition would be flawless and uncomplicated, with no one questioning his authority.

But Randolph wasn't here, and Lenora was seriously concerned that all hell was about to break loose in the Collingsworth clan. Not that either of her daughters would want any part of running the empire. Her youngest daughter, Jaime, avoided responsibility at any cost, sure it would lead to her immediate demise as a free spirit. And her older daughter, Becky, was far too busy holding a grudge against her estranged husband and trying to raise her twin seven-year-old sons to concern herself with business affairs.

Lenora's four sons were a different story. Langston, Matt, Bart and Zach each held their staunchly individual views of how Collingsworth Oil and the ranch itself should be run. Now, with their grandfather both mentally and physically incapacitated, she was afraid those differences would tear apart her close-knit family.

She turned at a rap on her bedroom door. "The old fart's here," Jaime announced, opening the door and stepping just near enough that Lenora could see that her skimpy blue shorts fit low on the hips, revealing lots of skin between them and the white blouse tied just below her breasts. "He said he's ready to start the meeting when you are."

"Thanks. Tell him I'll be right down." Nigel Slattery was not only the family attorney but an old and very dependable family friend.

"Don't hurry. Becky went upstairs to change clothes and she's not down yet."

"Speaking of changing clothes, you could exchange those shorts for a skirt or a pair of jeans. This *is* a business meeting, Jaime."

"It's in our dining room. Besides, a bunch of us are going down to the lake when we finish up here. Don't count on me for dinner. We'll be back late."

As usual. Late to bed and late to rise was Jaime's preferred lifestyle. She had changed majors so often that it had taken her six years to get a four-year degree in sociology, and then she had spent a year traveling in Europe to find herself before she started on a career. She was twenty-five now and the only job she'd pursued with any enthusiasm or longevity was spending the remainder of the trust from her late great-grandfather that she'd received on her twenty-first birthday.

Lenora took a last sip from her glass of iced tea and straightened the front of her denim skirt and white blouse before walking into the hall. Loud voices and boisterous laughter rang in her ears as she descended the winding staircase to the first floor. Her four sons would already be sitting around the massive oak table that overlooked the giant oaks that Jeremiah had planted the year he'd built the house for his wife.

The table, like the house itself, had been built to withstand the hot south-Texas summers and the hurricanes that blew in from the Gulf of Mexico. But it was the winds of change that threatened now, and Lenora wasn't sure even the Collingsworth blood that ran through all her children's veins could withstand that.

Langston was the first to his feet when she stepped through the door, and she noted that her older son had already taken over his grandfather's seat at the head of the table. She wondered what his brothers thought about that.

He kissed her on the cheek. "We thought for a minute you'd run out on the meeting."

"Now why would I do that?"

Matt pulled out her usual chair at the other end of the table. "Maybe because you hate business discussions."

"I like discussions. I don't like arguments."

"We never argue," Bart teased. "We just have heated dialogue until these guys come around to seeing things my way."

"Like that last brainstorm you had about inviting students from A&M out to run the spring roundup and branding," Matt said.

"Was it my fault they sent us coeds who got sick every time the iron touched the thick hide of a cow?"

"Hey, don't knock that experiment," Zach said. "I managed a few dates with that hot blonde before she decided to transfer back to UCLA and become an actress instead of a large-animal vet."

"Yep, little brother," Langston said. "You scared off another one."

Zach grinned. "Too much man for her."

Nigel Slattery ignored the brotherly camaraderie, opened his briefcase and laid a sheaf of papers on the table in front of him. "What's the latest word on Jeremiah?"

"The doctors claim he's progressing physically," Lenora said, "but he still just lies there staring into space. He shows no signs of recognizing any of us."

"Then he's obviously in no condition to continue as CEO of Collingsworth Enterprises, so I guess we should get started."

"Right," Jaime said. "Let's see what kind of little surprise Gramps has planned for us this time. He's probably decided we should go out and make our own fortune and given us thirty days to vacate the ranch."

"Not funny," Matt said. "In fact, I don't see why we have to bother with this at all. Langston and I are the oldest. By rights he should head the oil company as he's doing now and I should manage the ranch. We don't need a CEO over us."

"Whoa!" Bart said. "I don't know what age has to do with anything, and last time I checked we were co-managing the ranch."

"Sure. I wasn't trying to exclude you," Matt said. "Couldn't do it without you."

"Nice that you know that."

"Aren't you guys forgetting there's a fourth brother?" Zach said. "You know, the good-looking one."

Langston picked up a pen and scribbled on a notepad as if he were making notes. "I've got you covered, little brother. How's president of chasing women?"

"Works for me as long as it pays well. But if Mom is going to insist I drive to Houston and spend my days cooped up in an office, I expect to be more than a flunky."

Lenora studied her children as Nigel shuffled papers. Her sons had all inherited their father's good looks, all with his dark hair and eyes, classic nose and strong jaw line. Langston was a tough businessman, used to playing hardball with the movers and shakers in the oil business. He was far more sophisticated than the rest of her sons, and when he was dressed in one of his expensive suits as he was tonight, she found it hard to believe his roots were here on the ranch. That worried her. As did his recent engagement, which had seemed to come from out of the blue.

Her girls looked far more like her side of the family. Becky's hair was blond, streaked by hours spent in the sun with her boys. Jaime was a strawberry-blonde. Both were petite with fair skin and sky-blue eyes. The similarities ended there. If she hadn't given birth to both of them in this very house, she'd have sworn there had been a mixup at the hospital. Becky was athletic and a perfectionist, as unforgiving of shortcomings in others as she was in herself. Jaime was—Jaime.

Nigel cleared his throat. "I've made copies for all of you, but I thought I'd read it to you first."

"We can all read," Langston said.

"I know that. I just want to get it all said and done before you start complaining."

"I told you," Jaime said. "We'll be homeless by morning. Guess we'll have to move in that fancy penthouse with you, Langston."

"Celeste would love that," Zach said.

"How about we leave Celeste out of this?"

Lenora would love to second that, but she counted it good fortune enough that Langston's fiancée hadn't pushed her way into the night's meeting.

"I'll just skip to the meat of the matter," Nigel said. He waited until the room was dead-quiet before he started to read the chosen parts of what appeared to be a multi-paged document.

"My six grandchildren will one day inherit the Collingsworth fortune. I hope at that time they will be ready to assume full responsibility for running Jack's Bluff Ranch and Collingsworth Oil Company in a manner that would honor the land and the Collingsworth name."

Jaime's cell phone rang. She tugged it from the pocket of her shorts and was about to answer when Bart reached over and quietly slipped it from her fingers. She made a face at him but didn't protest further when he turned it off and handed it back to her.

Nigel looked to Lenora and something in the look multiplied tenfold the fear she'd been harboring. He took a drink from the glass of water at his elbow and adjusted his glasses.

"My grandchildren are clearly not ready to assume full responsibility yet."

"What the hell does that mean?" Matt said, glancing around the room for backup. "If he's thinking of bringing in some stranger to take over Jack's Bluff, it's not going to fly."

"Let him finish," Langston said, but his tone had taken on a wary edge.

"For that reason," Nigel said, pausing to look each of the Collingsworth siblings in the eye. "I feel it prudent to appoint my daughter-in-law, Lenora Collingsworth as acting CEO of Collingsworth Enterprises and assign her the final say in all major decisions affecting Collingsworth Oil and Jack's Bluff Ranch."

Langston pushed back from the table. "If this is some kind of joke, it isn't funny."

"Right," Bart said. "Gramps surely doesn't expect me to consult with Mom about improving beef production."

"Mom has no experience in the business realm," Matt said. "Running an oil company or a ranch is a far cry from chairing a committee for the symphony or raising funds for the homeless."

Becky threw up her hands. "It's ridiculous. What will people say if Mom goes back to work at her age? The boys need her here. We all need her here."

Jaime was laughing too hard to say anything.

Lenora fumed. She didn't want the added responsibility any more than they wanted her to have it, but it wasn't as if she was as old or as incapable as they made her out to be. They'd been born choking on a Collingsworth silver spoon. She hadn't. She'd gotten her first job at sixteen, though she had to admit working at a fast-food restaurant in Galveston hadn't prepared her for a CEO position.

"This is ludicrous," Langston said. "Gramps was

clearly out of his head when he had that drawn up. I'll make the decisions at Collingsworth Oil."

"And I'll continue to run the ranch as I see fit," Matt said.

Bart pushed his chair back from the table and stood. "Don't you mean as we see fit?"

Langston pushed up the sleeve of his pale gray dress shirt and looked at his watch. "I have to get back to Houston for a dinner engagement at eight, but I'll check my calendar tomorrow and call a meeting of the four of us to decide how to set up the new scheme of operations."

"The four of us?" Becky questioned. "There are six grandchildren."

"Why call a meeting?" Matt asked. "We're all here right now. I'm sure that Celeste can eat dinner on her own one night."

Acid pooled in Lenora's stomach, and she felt the old familiar ache that twenty-one years of loneliness hadn't erased. She needed Randolph here beside her. But he wasn't here, and she wouldn't see her family destroyed.

She stood and waited until she had everyone's attention. "I appreciate your concerns, but as of tonight, and until Jeremiah is well enough to take over again, I am the acting CEO of Collingsworth Enterprises. And I do not intend to hold the position in name only."

The shock of all six of her children was palpable. Nigel smiled. And Lenora feared she'd just made the biggest mistake of her life.

LANGSTON SWALLOWED A CURSE. This was all his fault. He was the eldest. He should have seen this coming and taken care of the issue before it reached the family table, or at least have handled things smarter tonight. He should have protected his mother instead of letting her be forced into a position she couldn't possibly handle.

He stared down the massive oak table at her as if seeing her for the first time. He didn't know when her hair had started graying or when the wrinkles around her eyes had grown deeper. In his mind she was still the mother who'd sat with him in the hospital after his first fall from a horse. The mother who'd driven him twenty miles to Little League practices and cheered him through every game.

She was Mom. *Not* a CEO.

"There are some legal issues we need to deal with," Nigel said. "And some paperwork to be signed before all this becomes official."

"We're not signing anything tonight," Langston said.

"Your signature isn't needed," Nigel said as he started to pass out copies of the document from which he'd been reading. "Only Lenora's signature is required."

The front doorbell rang. Jaime jumped up to run for the door. "I'll get it," Langston said, needing an escape. A double shot of scotch wouldn't hurt, either.

He opened the door and felt a blast of hot air and a rush of memories that almost knocked him off his feet. The teenage girl staring up at him had dark, curly hair and sweeping thick eyelashes over soft doelike eyes. The same hair. The same eyes as…

He loosed his necktie in a futile attempt to make breathing easier.

The girl shoved her hands into the front pockets of her denim cutoffs. "I'm looking for Langston Collingsworth."

"I'm Langston. Who are you?"

"My name's Gina Cantrell."

"Do I know you?"

"I think you know my mom. Trish Cantrell."

Trish's daughter. No wonder she looked so much like her, though the last name was different. But then it would be if she'd married and had a daughter.

"Do you know my mom or not?"

"Yeah, I know her." He looked around for an unfamiliar car. There was none, and he doubted she was old enough to have a license. "How did you get here?"

"On a Greyhound bus. The driver let me off at your gate."

Which was a good half mile from the house, and the temperature and humidity were both in the nineties. "Come in and cool off," he said. "I'll get you a cold soft drink and you can tell me what you're doing here."

She stepped past him. "I need your help."

"If you're running away from home, I can tell you right now that you've come to the wrong man."

"I'm not running away. It's my mother. She's…" Gina shuddered.

"What about your mother?"

"She's been abducted."

Trish. Abducted. His mind closed down for an agonizing second then darted recklessly to a thousand places he'd forbidden it to revisit.

"At least, she may have been kidnapped." Gina pulled away. She'd quit shaking, but she was staring at him, her eyes riveting and pleading. "I have to find her. Will you help me?"

The question bucked around inside him though the answer was a given. He could never turn his back on a woman in danger.

Chapter Two

Unwilling to involve the whole family in this until he had a better idea what he was dealing with, Langston had taken Gina to the screened back porch that served as the most popular gathering spot of the big house. Gina was perched in a wooden rocker, sipping from the tall glass of lemonade Lenora had pushed into her hand the second she saw how hot and sweaty the girl was. Langston took a seat opposite her on the wicker sofa, moving a few of the pillows so he could lean back.

Gina stared at him, and he sensed that it was not only fear but suspicion that shadowed her dark eyes. "How do you and my mother know each other?"

"We both worked for the same company when we were in college."

Her eyes narrowed. "And you haven't seen her since then?"

"That's right."

"I don't get it," Gina said. "If you haven't seen my mother in years, why would she tell me to come to you now?"

"I don't know, but if you tell me everything, maybe

we can figure this out together. Start at the beginning, and don't leave anything out."

"I don't know much. That's the problem—or at least one of the problems."

"What makes you think she's been abducted?"

Gina's hands shook, tinkling the ice in her glass. "Mom called me this morning."

"What time was that?"

"Eight minutes after ten, according to the record on my cell phone.

"Did it record the number she called from?"

"It was her cell phone, but when I tried to call her back, there was no answer."

Langston leaned in closer. "What did Trish say when she called?"

Gina shook her head. "I don't remember exactly, but she said I should *not* try to get in touch with her—or to call the police. She said that she'd call me again as soon as she could, but she didn't know when that would be."

Langston noticed the teenager's eyes were red-rimmed.

"Are you sure she said *not* to call the police?"

"I'm sure. I wanted to call 9-1-1, but then I was afraid to. I didn't know what to do except come here."

"Did Trish mention anyone's name?"

Gina shook her head again. "But she also talked to the camp supervisor and told her there was a family emergency, and that she needed someone to drive me to the nearest bus station so that I could go to a relative's home. When I got back on the phone, she told me to buy a ticket to Colts Run Cross and tell the driver to let me out at Jack's Bluff Ranch. She said he'd pass right by here on his route and that once I got here, I should stay until she could get in touch with me."

"But she didn't say she was in danger or that she'd been abducted?"

"No, but she hasn't called back. She knows I'm upset…but I can't reach her. That's not something my mom would do."

"Who's this camp supervisor you mentioned?"

"Ms. Bulligia. I'm working as a junior counselor in a summer camp south of Dallas. That's where we live—Dallas."

So Trish had moved back to Texas. He wondered when that had happened, not that it mattered. Their lives had gone different ways long ago—which made this all the more bizarre. "Is there a husband, other siblings?"

"No. My father's dead. There's just Mom and me. She owns a boutique, not far from our house."

"What about a boyfriend?"

"Me? Or Mom?"

"Your mom. Is there someone she might have had a fight with?"

"There's no boyfriend, at least not lately. She's off guys, 'cause they're jerks. This one guy used to come into the boutique to buy gifts for his wife, but he started hitting on Mom and then showing up everywhere she went."

"What happened with him?"

"She called the cops, and they scared him off."

So she did normally go to the cops, instead of telling her daughter not to call them. "When was that?"

"A year ago."

"And she hasn't been bothered by him since?"

"I don't think so."

Which didn't necessarily mean the man had lost his fascination for Trish. She was not an easy person to forget. Langston could definitely vouch for that. They sat without talking, with only the whir of the ceiling fan and the occasional whinny of a horse in a nearby pasture to break the silence.

"Think carefully, Gina. Did your mother say anything else when she called?"

"Only that…" Gina's voice broke completely and she hugged her arms around her chest. "She said that she loved me. That's the last thing she said before she hung up."

"Who did you tell that you were coming here?"

"No one."

"Not even a girlfriend?"

"No. I was afraid they'd call the police and make this worse for my mom." Gina shuddered. "I have to find her, but I don't know where to look. I don't know how to start." A tear spilled from her right eye and started to roll down her cheek. She brushed it away with the back of her hand.

Something tightened around Langston's chest like a lasso. He walked over and put a hand on Gina's shoulder. He was awkward at dealing with emotional females, always had been. "I'm not sure what's going on, but I'll find your mother, Gina. Count on it."

Gina jumped up from the rocker. "I'll go with you to look for her."

"No, you stay here at the ranch. You'll be safe and you'll be available if Trish tries to contact you again. But you can help."

"How?"

"Write down anything I should know. Home and boutique addresses. Names of employees at the boutique. Names and phone numbers of your mother's friends—male and female. The name of the stalker from last year. Where she goes when she wants some quiet time away from home. Anyplace you think she might go to hide."

He pulled a pen and small black notebook from the inside pocket of his suit jacket and handed them to her. "And I need a current picture of your mother if you have one. If not, write me out a good description."

"I have a picture of the two of us and Selena that we took before I left for camp."

"Who's Selena?"

"She works at the boutique, but she's also Mom's best friend."

"Be sure I have her name, address and phone number as well."

"When will you leave?"

"As soon as I can change into a pair of jeans and throw a few things together."

"I'll have the information ready." She looked up at him, eyes moist. "You must have been a very good friend for her to have sent me to you after all this time."

"Yeah, good friends." And that was all Gina needed to know.

He'd spent years trying not to think of Trish at all. He'd never fully succeeded. She'd always been there, skirting the back of his mind like a song that stayed in his head long after the music had stopped. Now the music was hitting crescendo again.

But this was only about finding Trish and making sure she was safe. Old songs—like old feelings—couldn't be trusted.

THE PLANNED FAMILY MEETING had dissolved, but a new one waited for Langston when he reached the kitchen, this one between him and his three brothers, who were all having beers and killing time until they could start interrogating him.

"What gives?" Matt asked.

"Do you remember Trish Edwards?"

"Yeah, I remember her."

"Gina is Trish's daughter, though the name's not Edwards now. It's Cantrell."

"What's her daughter doing here?"

"She thinks her mother's in some kind of trouble, that she may have been abducted." Langston filled his brothers in on the little he knew.

Zach straddled a straight-back chair. "So who is this mysterious Trish?"

Matt planted a hand on Zach's shoulder. "A woman who dumped your brother years ago."

"You've been dumped?" Zach asked. "Why have I missed out on this?"

"I was still in college," Langston said. "You were a mere snotty-nosed kid at the time."

"Exactly," Matt said, his tone edgy. "Trish was a long time ago. You don't owe her anything, and even if you did, this is police business. If there's been an abduction, they'll be able to handle it better than you."

"Like I said, Trish doesn't want police involvement, but I'll call them if it seems warranted."

"If you don't want go to the police," Bart said, "I know a great private detective in Houston. He does the legwork for Phil Caruthers and some of the other leading criminal defense lawyers in the city. There's no one he can't find."

"Write down his name and phone number for me," Langston said. "I may need him before this is over."

"So what are you going to do?" Zach asked.

"Drive to Dallas and see if I can figure out what's going on."

"Why not fly up in the company Cessna?" Zach asked. "It would be a lot quicker."

"I'll need the car when I get there, and there won't be that much traffic this time of the night. I can make the drive in under four hours."

"I still say call the cops," Matt said. "You don't even know the woman anymore. She could be involved with drugs or wanted for something and on the run."

"She owns a boutique. That's not your typical criminal profile."

"If I can't talk sense into you, I'll go with you," Matt said. "Bart can handle the ranch a few days without me."

"And if I can't, I have CEO Mother to tell me what to do."

Matt groaned. "That is not a joking matter."

"I'd rather go this alone at first," Langston said. "I can keep a lower profile that way, but I'll call if it looks like I need assistance."

Bart nodded. "What about Gina?"

"I'd appreciate it if you'd take responsibility for her. I don't want her to leave the ranch unless you're with her. And all of you will need to be on guard that no one comes looking for her and causes any trouble at the ranch."

"That's a given," Matt said.

"Are you going to explain all of that to Mom?" Bart asked.

"That's my next order of business. Then I'll pack a few things and hit the road."

"If you don't have what you need, help yourself to my closet," Bart said. "The jeans and shirts should fit. I don't know about the shoes. I've got man feet, you know."

"If the man's a giant," Zach mocked.

"I keep some old jeans and boots and such at the big house so that I don't have to pack a duffel every time I drive out," Langston said. "They'll do."

"Anything I can do to help, just say the word," Zach said. "I'm your man."

"How would you like to escort Celeste to a dinner party at Mayor Griffin's tonight?"

Zach groaned. "Let me rephrase that offer. Anything I can do for you short of riding a maniacal bull or spending an evening with your charming fiancée, just let me know."

"And she speaks so highly of you."

"Yeah, right."

None of his brothers were particularly fond of Celeste, but that would change when they got to know her better. He was sure of it. Langston headed off to find his mother and was already at the top of the stairs when Matt caught up with him.

"You'll need a handgun," Matt said. "You can take my Glock."

"Thanks."

Matt put a hand on Langston's arm. "You don't have to do this, you know."

"Sure I do. When has a Collingsworth ever turned their back on a woman in distress?"

"Never, but I'm not sure that's what this is about. If it's about some kind of bond you think you have with Trish, just remember that the two of you were a hell of a long time ago. You've changed a lot in those years. She will have to. You can't just go back and pick up where you left off, not even if…"

"I have no plans to pick up anything. I'm engaged. I just need to check this out. That's all."

"Sure." Matt delivered a brotherly punch to the arm. "Just be careful, bro."

"I always am."

LENORA WAS IN SEMI-SHOCK by the developments of the meeting with Nigel and then with the idea of Langston rushing off to north Texas to rescue an old girlfriend. But she could see how Gina's story would have gotten to him. The girl was scared to death.

"This will be your room," Lenora said, leading Gina into the guest room on the far eastern end of the upstairs hall.

Gina looked around for a few seconds before dropping her one piece of luggage to the bed. "Did you know my mom well?"

"Not well, but I've met her. She wasn't a lot older than you at the time."

"Did she come here to Jack's Bluff Ranch?"

"Several times. She loved the horses, could never wait to go riding."

"She still likes to ride, but she doesn't get to do it much. We live in the city."

Gina walked to the window and stared out. The view looked directly over the garden that they'd built around the rosebush Randolph had given Lenora for their first anniversary. Beyond that was a stretch of pines that gave away quickly to open pasture.

It was almost six, but the sun was still high enough in the sky for the roses to show off their beautiful collage of colors. Dark came late in July.

"Mom never mentioned any of you," Gina said. "I don't know why she sent me here."

"I couldn't say," Lenora said, "but delightful young ladies are always welcome at Jack's Bluff."

"Thanks."

"The bathroom is down the hall, the second door to your left. Normally you'd have to share it with the twins, my seven-year-old grandsons who have the room across the hall from you, but David and Derrick are with their father for two more weeks."

"I won't be here two weeks. I'll be leaving as soon as my mom's okay." She walked back to the bed and unzipped her bag. "How many people live in this house?"

"Currently six, seven counting you."

"Does Langston live here?"

"No, he lives in Houston. And Matt and Bart have their own houses here on the ranch. Zach, Jaime and Becky—the twins' mother—all live here in the big house."

"You have a large family."

"Yes, I do. You met all of them except the twins. How about you, Gina? Do you have brothers and sisters?"

"No. It's just me and my mom." Gina started to unpack, but stopped and collapsed on the bed.

"There's plenty of time to shower and take a nap before dinner," Lenora said. "We won't eat until seven-thirty. Juanita's making a chicken enchilada casserole, at least that's my name for it. It's spicy, but superb."

"Who's Juanita?"

"Our cook. Bart hired her last year, because he and the boys wanted me to take it a little easier. Actually, I miss my kitchen and I'm a little jealous sometimes that she gets the compliments instead of me."

"Then why don't you fire her?"

"I can't. She makes tamales to die for. Besides, it gives me more time for my charity work and spending time with my grandsons." And now time to exert some influence into the operations of Collingsworth Enter-prises—or at least into the development of her sons and even her daughters.

Gina kicked out of her shoes. "I'd like a shower, but I can't really dress for dinner. All I have with me are shorts and T-shirts."

"They'll do fine. I tried the policy of dressing for dinner for awhile. I gave it up after I got tired of sitting at the table by myself. Now we're back to South Texas rules. Come as you are, but the horse and spurs stay outside."

Gina finally smiled.

Lenora did, too, though a sudden horrifying thought crept into her mind. Suppose Trish wasn't all right. Suppose Langston was too late and something had gone terribly wrong.

Maybe she should call Billy Mack. He had a friend that had been a Texas Ranger before he retired. Langston might not appreciate her calling their neighbor in on this, but Billy was older and had a level head on him. And he'd been a friend of the Collingsworth family all his life.

If Langston didn't call back with good news by morning, she might just give Billy a call. Lenora forced a smile and left the room quickly before Gina saw her fear. The girl had more than enough of her own.

LANGSTON HIT THE ACCELERATOR of his sleek black Porsche as he pulled out of the gate of Jack's Bluff and headed north. No matter what Matt said, this wasn't about his old relationship with Trish. Those feelings were dead, had been for years. He might have thought he'd loved Trish once, but what had he known of love at nineteen?

Yet the old memories began to haunt his mind. Slow dancing with Trish in Cutter's Bar. Watching her float along the surface of the water when they'd gone skinny-dipping in the moonlight. Holding Trish in his arms. Tasting her lips.

His muscles grew taut as a new wave of adrenaline rushed through his veins. Trish was in danger and she needed him. That's all he'd deal with now.

Chapter Three

It was ten-thirty by the time Langston pulled up in front of Trish's home in a fashionable section of west Dallas. There were lights in most of the houses, but Trish's was dark except for the landscaping lamps dotted about the flowerbeds and shrubbery. The house was two-story with lots of angles and gables on a corner lot. Langston parked in the driveway and killed the engine. He'd made a few phone calls on his way north. One had been to Aidan Jefferies, a detective friend in Houston who'd learned that Trish had been involved in a carjacking/kidnapping incident eight days ago.

Luckily she'd escaped unhurt after being rescued by a local detective, a man who'd become suspicious when he spotted the car speeding down an Interstate exit ramp and recognized the abductor as a suspect he'd questioned months earlier. The detective had followed until Trish had run the car off the road and wrecked the car. A shootout had followed, and the carjacker had been shot and killed by the cop. It had made the local newspaper but not the front page. An explosion at a local plant had been the hot topic of the day.

An open-and-shut case according to police records, but Langston had a strong suspicion that it was somehow tied to the strange phone call she'd made to Gina.

He retrieved his emergency flashlight from his glove compartment and stuck it in the front pocket of his jeans. He also took the Glock, just to be on the safe side. He rang the bell and waited. As expected, there was no answer and no signs of life.

Breaking in houses wasn't his specialty, though this wouldn't officially be breaking and entering since Gina had given him her key. He put his face to the door and shot a beam of light into the foyer.

He couldn't see much of the living area beyond the entranceway, but he did see an overturned table and a shattered vase, its bouquet of flowers scattered about the floor. His worry about alarms vanished.

He unlocked the door hurriedly and stepped inside. "Trish." He called her name but didn't wait for an answer before racing to the living room and then reeling at the destruction. Cushions and pillows were ripped and cotton and feathers were scattered everywhere.

Adrenaline rush and apprehension had his heart pounding as he made his way through the house. "Trish, it's Langston. Are you here? If you're hiding, you can come out." There was no response.

The rest of the house matched the kitchen. Drawers were open, their contents scattered. Even the closets had been ransacked. Not your typical random vandalism. Whoever had come in was more likely looking for something in particular. He tried the kitchen door that led to the garage. It was unlocked and the garage was empty.

He stepped over broken glass and walked to the door

that led from the kitchen to the backyard, flicking on the outside light and stepping outside. There was a small pool and some yard chairs. The area was enclosed by thick shrubbery and a high security fence. He spun and aimed the gun at the sound of movement in the water, but it was only the pool cleaner rearing its vacuuming head to spit a stream of water in his direction.

Langston scanned the pool. A plastic float was backed into the far right corner and a couple of iridescent diving rings rested on the bottom. The courtyard area was untouched by the demolition. He went back inside and searched again, not breathing easy until he was certain that Trish was not in the house, injured—or worse.

Leaving things just as he'd found them, Langston went back to his car, input the address that Gina had supplied into his GPS system and drove the few blocks to Trish's shop, Cottage Boutique. He stopped a couple of doors down, in a strip mall to the right of Trish's shop. The boutique looked more like an old house, a survivor in the world of sleek shopping centers. To the left was another cottage, this one a day spa spouting a sign that proclaimed it a haven from stress.

Trish's boutique was closed, as were all the shops except for a chain coffee café at the far end of the strip mall. He studied the displays of fashionably dressed mannequins in two lighted bay windows of the boutique as he walked to the front door. Thick drapes hung behind the displays, keeping the shop's interior from view.

The door was locked and the blinds were closed tight so that there was no way to see inside. A small sign by the doorway said Please Ring For Entry. He did. The shop stayed dark and silent.

Frustrated, he pulled the list of names and numbers Gina had given him from his pocket and held it beneath the beam of his flashlight. The photograph of Selena, Gina and Trish stared back at him. His chest tightened and his lungs closed around his quickened breath. His instincts screamed that Trish was in trouble and that if he didn't find her fast, it would be too late.

He scanned the notes for the information on where Trish went when she needed to get away. Long walks in the park. Movies. A fishing camp on Lake Livingston that belonged to Selena's boyfriend. If she was running from someone, she might have gone there.

Langston was already back in his sports car when the lights in the front windows of the boutique flicked off. Probably on a timer he decided, but he waited for a few minutes to make certain. He'd started the engine and was backing from his parking spot when he saw the garage door of Trish's shop begin to lift.

Damn. There had been someone inside.

He revved his engine and swerved from the strip center, pulling into the driveway of the cottage just as a white compact car started to back out. The driver squealed to a stop when she saw him. He blocked her in, then jumped from behind the wheel and raced to her door.

He shone a beam of light into her car. The dark-haired young woman—the same one who was in the picture Gina had given him—stared at him, her eyes wide with fear.

He laid the pistol on top of the car, and leaned against the door. "I'm not going to hurt you, Selena," he said, talking loudly enough for her to hear through the closed window. "I'm looking for Trish Cantrell."

She shook her head.

"I didn't have anything to do with the carjacking. I'm just a friend. Gina came to me for help. My name's Langston Collingsworth." Not that there was any reason she'd have ever heard of him. Still, he took his wallet from his pocket and pressed his ID against the window, shining his light so that she could see it.

Surprisingly, she responded with a nod and some of the fear seemed to dissolve from her face as if she recognized his name.

"Can you lower the window so we can talk?"

She nodded and did as he'd asked. "Where's Gina? Is she okay?"

"At my family's ranch down in Colts Run Cross. She's fine but worried about her mother."

No response.

"Where's Trish?" he demanded.

"I don't know."

He leaned closer. "I know Trish is in trouble. I know about the carjacking and I've seen the mess at her house."

"How could you know about the carjacking?" she asked suspiciously. "Gina doesn't even know about that."

"It's not exactly a secret. It was in the newspaper and I talked to a friend who's a detective."

"You talked to the police?"

"I talked to one cop. He's not with the DPD. Trish is obviously in danger, and Gina came to me. I just want to help."

"I don't know where she is. Now, please, move your car. I have to go home."

He grabbed her arm. "Is she at your boyfriend's fishing cabin?"

"I don't know what you're talking about."

"You're lying. She's at the camp, isn't she?"

"If I tell you, you must promise not to go to the police, not even to your detective friend."

"Why?"

"I don't know. But Trish made me promise on the Bible, and you have to promise, too."

He didn't make promises easily, and he never broke them unless he found out he'd been lied to. This time he had no choice. There was no time to waste. "I don't have a Bible on me, but I'll give you my word as a Collingsworth and that's just as sacred a promise."

"It better be. She said she might go to the camp. That's all I know. I haven't heard from her since last night after someone broke into her house."

Too bad he hadn't known that before he'd driven all the way to Dallas. "I need better directions than Gina gave me. There's no time to waste looking for the place."

"Okay, but you have to help her. If you don't, he's going to kill her."

"Who?"

"I don't know." Her fear was palpable, and it crawled inside him, adding a sense of urgency that set his nerves even more on edge as she hurriedly scribbled the directions on the back of what looked like a gasoline receipt.

She pressed the note into his hand. "Make sure you're not followed."

"Count on it."

"All I know about you, Langston Collingsworth, is that when Trish talks about you, it's as if you are some kind of friggin' prince. So be one now. Don't let her down."

He swallowed hard as she pressed the note into his hand. He didn't bother with a goodbye, but just rushed back to his car, started the engine and jerked it into Reverse. He wasn't a prince, but he'd stack a cowboy against royalty any day.

As long as he wasn't already too late.

TRISH STOOD AT THE BACK DOOR of the rustic cabin and stared at the silvery bands of moonlight dancing across the lake. A light breeze stirred the leaves of a sweetgum tree, and an owl called down from one of its branches. Another time she would have found the isolation of the camp peaceful and inspiring. Tonight it only intensified the desperate fears that had driven her here.

If any of this made sense, she'd have a clearer idea what to do. She couldn't just stay here, hiding out as if she were the criminal. But she couldn't go back to Dallas, either, not until she knew what she was up against. And she definitely couldn't go to the cops.

Neither could Gina. So now she was at Colts Run Cross, in the last place Trish would have ever expected to send her. But desperation made a person take desperate risks.

Trish stepped outside. It was warm, but not the same kind of unforgiving heat that attacked Dallas so mercilessly in July and August. Credit the wind blowing across the lake for that.

The moon slid behind a cloud, turning the night pitch-dark. The high-pitched chorus of what must have been thousands of tree frogs filled the night, accompanied by the occasional screech of an owl and the rustle of grass as one of the night creatures hunted nearby.

Deer, squirrel, raccoon, skunks, armadillos—and snakes. She had lots of company. And she was totally alone.

A mosquito buzzed her face and landed on her cheek. She slapped it away, started to go back inside—then stopped dead-still as a new noise wafted on the breeze. It was a car engine. Fear slammed her senses. The man had found her. He'd make his demands again, and when she couldn't deliver…

The car came closer. She'd parked her rental at the edge of the wooded area, hidden from view so no one would know she was here. Big mistake since there was no way she could get to it now in time to escape.

Still she had to try.

She rushed in the house to get the keys, then took off out the back door again just as the car stopped in front of the house.

She'd have to go through the woods if there were any chance of not walking right into his hands. The brush hit her in the face and her footsteps sounded like a herd of deer as she raced through the heavy undergrowth. He had to hear her, and he'd be right behind her. The outline of her car was in view when a prickly branch snagged her jeans and sent her crashing to the damp carpet of pine straw. The keys flew from her hands.

She felt for them in the dark, imagining that any second her fingers would rake the body of a slithering snake instead. Only now she could hear footsteps. The man was right behind her. Leaving the keys, she stood and started running again, this time deeper into the woods.

"Trish."

The moon reappeared and filtered through the trees

enough that Trish could finally see where she was going. She tried to run faster, but stumbled. Her fingers scratched and slid along the rough bark of a tree trunk. And then she felt the man's body as he tackled her and they both went crashing to the ground.

"What the hell are you doing?"

She tried to roll over, but his body was pressing into hers and holding her down. "I don't have…" Finally she'd wiggled around enough to see the man's face, and her angry protests turned to cotton in her mouth. Her heart skipped erratically and then slammed against her chest.

"How did you find me?"

LANGSTON STARED INTO TRISH'S eyes, aware of the feel of his body pressing into hers, aware of his hands still wrapped around her waist, his fingers splayed against the bare flesh of her stomach beneath the loose T-shirt. Aware of her hair, in complete disarray with pine straw jutting from the dark curls.

A crazy jolt of arousal shot through him. He pushed away instantly.

She stood and brushed herself off. "What are doing here, Langston?"

"Nice to see you again, too, Trish. You really should work on your greeting skills, though."

"My greeting skills are fine when I'm expecting company. I wasn't. And you didn't answer my question. What are you doing here?"

"Looking for you. Your daughter is frantic."

"Is she with you?"

"No, she's at the ranch. What the devil is going on?"

"I'm not sure, but I think the cop who saved me from a carjacker last week is trying to kill me."

"Why would he?"

"I know it doesn't make sense, but he wants a video that he thinks I have."

"A video?"

"See, I told you it doesn't make sense."

To say the least. "Let's go inside and you can give me the full story."

"I'm not sure it's safe to be here with me. He could show up any minute."

"Then you'd better talk fast."

Not that he was going anywhere. There was no way he could walk away from her as long as she needed him.

But there wasn't a chance he'd let her sneak back into his heart.

Chapter Four

Trish had been totally unnerved before Langston arrived on the scene. Now it was worse. Langston wasn't the same youthful, high-flying college guy he'd been that hot, sultry summer in Houston. She wasn't the same naively optimistic woman she'd been. Still, the past seemed to dominate the situation and sensual tension charged the air.

Langston leaned against the kitchen counter, his piercing, dark eyes boring into hers. "Tell me about the carjacking."

Trish pulled a sprig of pine straw from her hair, dropped to one of the worn kitchen chairs and propped her elbows on the table. "I'd gone to lunch with one of the sales reps from my favorite jewelry line, but had taken my own car so I could stop by the drugstore on the way back to the boutique. I was still buckling up when some guy opened the passenger side door and jumped in."

"Buck Rivers."

"Right. How did you know that?"

"A friend told me, but that's about all I know. The

guy must have been watching you when you exited the restaurant."

"I guess, but I didn't see him. If I had, I wouldn't have thought anything about it. The parking lot was crowded and it was the middle of the day. And he was just a normal-looking guy—except for the pistol he pointed at my head."

"Go on."

"He was yelling at me to drive faster and ordering me when and where to turn. At first I thought he was just desperate to get somewhere and thought he might actually let me go after that. Once he forced me to turn on a deserted back road, I got a lot more worried."

"Did he act as if he knew you?"

"He just referred to me as a rich bitch. When he told me to stop, I panicked and hit the gas instead. He tried to kick my foot off the accelerator. That's when we left the blacktop. We were headed right for a bridge. I hit the ravine just before I hit the railing."

Langston joined her at the table. "You're lucky to be alive."

She looked up and let her eyes meet his. His gaze was still piercing, but shadowed now. She dropped her eyes and focused on his hands. No longer the hands of a rancher, she noticed. They were smooth. And there was no wedding ring on his left hand. It didn't matter. She couldn't let it.

"I wasn't hurt in the wreck other than sore muscles and a few bruises. The carjacker didn't have on his seat belt and was knocked out when his head hit the side window. A car pulled up and stopped on the side of the road. I thought he'd just happened by and saw the wreck, but it was an off-duty detective."

"Gary Packard."

She nodded. "He said he'd seen us speeding reck-lessly down the exit ramp when we left the highway. He thought I was drunk, then got close enough that he rec-ognized my abductor as someone he'd questioned before."

"So he followed you?"

"Right, but he didn't see the pistol pressing into my rib cage and didn't realize I'd been abducted. He just wanted to see what we were up to."

"How did he come to kill Rivers instead of arresting him?"

"Buck Rivers came to while I was explaining the situa-tion to the detective. He took off running and Detective Packard gave chase. I ran to the car, retrieved my cell phone from my handbag and made a 9-1-1 call. When I heard gunfire, I panicked again and hid in the woods until a state trooper responding to my call showed up."

"So you didn't see the shootout?"

"No. The detective came wandering out of the woods after the trooper arrived. He said he'd shot the carjacker in self-defense."

"How did you go from saved by a cop to thinking he is trying to take you out?"

"I'd like to know that myself. We hung around for a long time while the detective and the trooper searched the area. I guess they were looking for clues. Then when I refused to go to the hospital, the detective drove me back into town, asking questions the whole way. I had the feeling even then that he didn't really believe I was a random victim."

"Meaning?"

"I think he still thought I might have willingly been with Rivers. But he let it go and dropped me off at the car rental agency to get a replacement vehicle. He said mine would be towed, impounded and searched for clues even though the detective had spent a lot of time searching it while we were at the scene."

"What kind of clues? They already knew who abducted you and he was dead."

"I don't know. I didn't argue with him. I was still in shock at that point and just glad it was over. At least I thought it was over. Turned out I was badly mistaken. I got a phone call the next day demanding I return the video that Buck Rivers had left with me. When I told the caller I didn't have it, he called me a few obscene names and said if I was lying, I was dead."

"Did the caller give his name?"

"No. But when he first called I would have sworn I was talking to Detective Packard, but that he had a cold or something."

"What did you do?"

"I called Packard and told him about it. Then he questioned me about having a video. I'm not sure he believed that I didn't. But then he blew the whole thing off and said if there was no video then it was probably a crank call and that I should ignore it unless I heard from the man again. I didn't hear from him so I thought I was home-free."

"And then someone broke into your house last night."

"Selena told you?"

"No, I went to your place first. It's trashed."

"My house is trashed?"

"Didn't you know?"

"No. I left rather quickly after I rammed a screwdriver into the intruder's face."

"Keep talking."

She explained the situation as best she could. It had all happened so fast that she was short of facts.

"Why didn't you call the cops once you got away instead of coming here to hide out?"

She hesitated. Selena had thought she was paranoid. Langston would likely think she was plain crazy, but... "I think Gary Packard was the man who broke in my house."

"You couldn't tell?"

"He was wearing a ski mask. Look, I know this sounds crazy, but when I saw the intruder, I thought it was the detective. He had the same build, the same voice, but more gruff—like he was trying to disguise it, the same as the man had sounded on the phone."

"You can't just accuse a cop of trying to kill you, Trish."

"I know that." Her frustration level skyrocketed. "But I can't ignore all my instincts, either."

Langston nodded and pushed back from the table. "It's too late to try to figure this out tonight, but I'll make a few calls and get some men on it first thing in the morning."

"There's no reason for you to get involved in this, Langston."

"You asked for my help."

"I did no such thing."

"You sent Gina to me."

"I was hoping you'd keep her safe while I got this figured out. I didn't mean for you to come looking for me."

He stood as if the conversation were finished. "Sorry to disappoint you."

"Langston, you really don't have to get involved. I'm handling this."

"You're hiding in the woods. That was a wise escape plan. It's not a solution."

He'd been cocky at nineteen. He was downright bossy now. But he was right, She didn't have a plan and had no clue how to come up with one. She'd faced a lot in her life, but at least before, the cops had been the good guys.

He looked about the cabin. "Is there anything around here to eat?"

"Apples and potato chips that I picked up when I stopped to get gas. Fortunately, I got out of the house with my purse. That was it, except for the clothes I had on and my keys."

"Which makes me doubly glad I raided Mom's refrigerator before I left." Langston took his cell phone from the leather holder at his waist and tossed it to her. "Call your daughter and tell her you're safe while I get the groceries out of the car. She's worried sick about you."

"I've already tried to use my cell phone. There's no service out here."

"Mine's satellite. It will work. The number's programmed in under Mom."

Mom. Jack's Bluff. Names Trish remembered from years ago. The Collingsworths were a strong Texas family with wealth and political influence. That was Langston's reality.

And if she let him into her life, if he found out the truth about her and her past, that reality might become her destruction. So no matter how tempting it might be to let him come to her rescue, it was a risk she couldn't afford.

IT WAS TEN AFTER TWO in the morning, and Langston was yet to close his eyes or even to lie down. He really wanted to believe Trish, but her story was full of serious holes. The biggest was how this mystery video was supposed to have fallen into her hands. Did the cop, or whoever had trashed her house, think that the carjacker had hidden it in her car before he dashed into the woods never to return again? Not likely. And even if he had, the car wasn't in her possession. It had been towed away from the scene and impounded by the police.

He had to consider the possibility that Trish knew more than she was saying and that she might be lying about her relation—or lack of one—with Buck Rivers. His cell phone rang and he jumped to get it before it woke Trish. He whispered a hello.

"Langston, are you okay?"

Celeste. Damn. He was supposed to have called her hours ago. He stepped out on the front porch so that he could talk at normal volume. "I'm fine."

"I was worried sick about you. Why didn't you call me back?"

"I was tied up, and then it was too late. I didn't want to wake you."

"What's going on with that Trish person?"

That Trish person. She said it as if it was some kind of annoyance, like bad breath or a flat tire. He wished he'd never even mentioned Trish's name to her, but he'd owed her an explanation for running out on her tonight. He hadn't mentioned that Trish was an old girlfriend. He wasn't sure why except that it had been so long ago.

"If there's even a chance she's been abducted, you

should call the police and let them handle it," Celeste urged.

"She wasn't abducted."

"How do you know that?"

"I've located her."

"Then why did she send her daughter to you?"

"It's a long story, Celeste, and I'm dead-tired. I'll call you in the morning and give you a full update."

"Okay, but I still don't see why you went rushing off to Dallas just because some kid yelled wolf. It's probably just a scam to get money out of you."

"We'll talk in the morning."

"Not too early. I may sleep in. The dinner party didn't break up until nearly midnight. Melvin was nice enough to fill in for you at the last minute, and he and I went out for drinks after that. Just call when you get to the office."

Thank goodness for Melvin. Not only was he Langston's most valued VP at the company, but he was also always willing to pinch-hit when Langston couldn't make one of Celeste's social events. That was more than his brothers would do.

"I won't call too early," he promised. They said their goodnights and Langston broke the connection. Tired as he was, he didn't go back inside. Instead he stood on the edge of the narrow porch and stared into the shadows that played around the cabin.

He wasn't sure of the real answer to Celeste's question about why he'd come running to Dallas but he was glad he had. He'd always needed closure with Trish. Hopefully this would provide it, and he could finally get past the memories of that summer and the two of them reveling in their exploding hormones and thinking it was the real thing.

Sure, he'd had a brief relapse tonight, but that was just the memories and seeing her again after so long a time. He'd see Trish through this, and then he'd go on with his life without a backward glance.

He went back into the house and into the hall to get a pillow from the closet. He passed the bedroom where she was sleeping and hesitated, his senses suddenly intoxicated by her presence. He listened to her breathing and imagined her head resting on the pillow, her hair disheveled with the curls dancing about her cheeks.

He took a deep breath and stepped away. Tomorrow he'd be fine.

Tonight, the memories held sway.

SELENA ARRIVED AT THE BOUTIQUE at six minutes before nine the next morning, though it didn't open until ten and she'd stayed late to do paperwork last night. Her boyfriend's truck was in the shop and she had to drive him to work for eight-thirty. Once she was out, she figured she may as well go to work herself.

Selena went back to the kitchen and started a pot of coffee. Once the brew was dripping, she made a quick tour of the shop, checking each room to make sure it was ready for business. She saved the blue room for last. It was her favorite. The furnishings were the same type of beautiful antiques as in the rest of the cottage, but it was in the style of a privileged lady's boudoir.

Selena never tired of laying the silky lingerie across the huge four-poster bed or displaying it in the magnificent, mahogany wardrobe. Not to mention that the white lace and satin bridal set she'd hung next to the eighteenth century washstand practically made her mouth water.

When she and Enrico married, she planned to wear one like that on her honeymoon. Then no matter how many times they'd made love before, she'd feel like a princess bride. She knew he loved her, but he wanted to save money for a down payment on a house before they set the date. But it would be soon. His bank account was growing fast.

Today, even thinking about that didn't lift her troubled spirits. She started back to the business office, then paused when she thought she heard someone in the front room of the shop.

Just her jagged nerves, she decided, since even during business hours the doors to the outside stayed locked. Customers rang the doorbell as if entering the house of a friend. Trish claimed that was part of the boutique's charm and made it feel far more exclusive.

Selena dropped to the computer and pulled up the list of customers to be notified that the new shipment of Jimmy Choo shoes was going on display August fourth. But there was that noise again, only closer. She spun around in the chair as the man stepped into the doorway behind her, one hand resting on the doorframe, the other behind his back.

"Nice little setup you've got here."

"Who are you? How did you get in?"

"I came by to do some shopping. Where's Trish?"

Oh, no! Fear settled like red-hot coals in her chest. She reached for the button beneath her desk that sent a silent alarm to the police, turning her body so that he wouldn't see her fingers. "Trish isn't here."

"I can see that. Where is she?"

"I don't know."

"I kind of think you might." He pulled the hand from behind his back and pointed the barrel of a stubby black pistol at her head. "Where's Trish?"

Her stomach rolled and Selena tried to swallow through the hard, dry crust that her throat had become. "I told you I don't know where she is." Her words were so shaky she wasn't even sure they were intelligible.

He inched closer, his hand steady and his finger sliding to the trigger. "I'm counting to three. If you don't happen to remember by then where I can find your boss lady, you won't be remembering anything ever again. And if you lie to me, I'll track you down and yank your heart out through your throat."

"Why are you doing this?"

"One."

She didn't want to die. She wanted to wear the beautiful bridal lingerie. Wanted to marry Enrico. Wanted to have his children. "This is about that video isn't it? Trish doesn't have your stupid video."

"Two."

She heard a siren. The cops were on the way.

"Three."

LANGSTON'S CELL PHONE RANG at nine-thirty the next morning. The ID read Aidan Jefferies. Good. He knew he could count on his detective buddy to work quickly. "Any luck?"

"Some. Gary Packard's got a clean record except for one count of domestic violence against his wife. That was ten years ago. They've divorced since."

"What about Buck Rivers?"

"He's been in Dallas for four years and has had several arrests—no convictions. He always seems to be around trouble, but there's never any proof that he's in it. He's been working as a bouncer at one of the local gentleman's clubs for the past six months. One of the dancers reported he'd beaten her up a month ago, but later recanted the charges. There's probably a lot more on him, but that was all I could get with phone calls to the DPD. I'll follow up, but I could fax that to you if you'd like hard copy."

"We barely have indoor plumbing here." He stepped outside the door so that Trish wouldn't overhear his next question. "Did you get any information on Trish Cantrell?"

"She bought the Cottage Boutique five years ago after moving to the States from London. No police record. Not even an unpaid parking ticket. So are you heading back to Houston today?"

"That's the plan. I'll give you a call later." He thanked Aidan again, broke the connection and went back inside.

Trish had showered and was dressed in the same clothes she'd had on last night. The shorts showed off her tan and terrific thighs and the pale pink T-shirt fit just snug enough to cup beneath her breasts. Her hair was still damp but curling about her cheeks.

He forced his gaze away. The close quarters were definitely getting to him. "I could use some break-fast," he said.

"I still have an apple."

"I'm thinking more like bacon and eggs."

"I could go for that. I'm starved, and I actually got some sound sleep last night for the first time since the carjacking."

"Good."

"And I've made some decisions." She propped her bottom on the arm of the faded sofa. "I'll hire a private investigator to look into the mystery tape and a body-guard to protect me until I know exactly who's behind all of this."

And just like that he'd be out of her life again. He should feel relieved, but his knee-jerk reaction felt more like a punch to the gut. "What about Gina?"

"I'll hire a bodyguard for her, too. Now shall we go somewhere and find breakfast? I'd like to head back to Dallas as soon as possible."

His cell phone ran. Aidan, again. He took the call.

"Breaking news," Aidan said. "I just heard from a friend with the DPD that Selena Hernandez's body was found minutes ago inside the Cottage Boutique. She was shot twice in the head at close range. A cop found her when he answered a silent alarm she'd apparently set off before she was shot."

"Sonofabitch."

"Yeah. Looks like Trish Cantrell is playing with some real sweet guys. I'll get back to you as soon as I hear anything else."

Langston was trying to decide how to break the news to Trish when his phone rang again. This time it was Celeste. He let it ring. She'd never understand why he was bringing an old girlfriend involved with a killer home with him.

Chapter Five

Trish fought the panic. This was a nightmare, a horrible terrifying nightmare that she'd wake from any second. Only she didn't wake, not even when she stepped out of her shoes and into the shallow water at the lake's edge and her toes sank into the mud.

She stared out at the lake as the sun beat down on her back and the weight of the humid air clogged her lungs. A hand pressed into her shoulder. She didn't bother to turn around. "Get out of here, Langston, while you still can. I had no right to pull you into my problems."

"It's a little late to think about that."

Finally she met his burning gaze. "Just go, please. Just go."

"I'm afraid I can't do that."

"You can. You should." Her voice broke and the tears she'd been fighting welled in her eyes.

"I don't run out on a task just because it gets tough. But you have to level with me. I have to know the whole truth."

The anger hit hard, knocking her from the state of semi-shock. "I have told you the truth, Langston. I've told everyone the truth. And I never asked for you to take this on." The anger meshed with the heartache over Selena, and she gave up on fighting the tears. They poured from her eyes and slid down her face. Trembling, she turned back to stare at the lake.

Langston shed his own shoes, rolled up his jeans and joined her in the water. "Take it easy. I'm trying to understand, but that carjacking story is a little hard to swallow."

"Go to hell, Langston Collingsworth."

"Look, I'm sorry if I sound doubtful. I'm just trying to get a handle on this."

She tried to pull away from him, but he tightened his grip on her shoulders, pulling her close and then circling his arms around her. The sobs tore from her throat, and she fell against him, hating that she needed him, yet holding on as he rocked her in his arms.

He didn't say anything else, and she didn't have the energy to argue. When she finally stopped crying, he loosed his grip and took her hand, leading her back toward the cabin.

"I have to go back to Dallas," she said. "I have to see Selena's boyfriend. Enrico will fall apart when he gets the news. They were so in love."

"Going back to Dallas is not a good idea."

"It's where I live. And there's the boutique. I have to check on it."

"I can have someone go to the shop and put up a Closed sign. The cops probably have it staked off with crime scene tape anyway, and I'm sure they'll be looking for you by now."

She shuddered. "To talk to me, or to kill me?"

"Hopefully just to talk, and, remember, you don't

have any real proof that Gary Packard was the guy who broke into your house. You admitted he had on a mask that hid all his facial features."

"So what do you think I should do?"

"Talk to a lawyer."

Her head spun. She didn't need a lawyer. This was all some horrible mistake, what Selena would call… But Selena was dead. The pain gripped her again, leaving her so shaken she could barely think. "I have to call Enrico."

"You can call him, but I think it's best if you don't tell anyone that you'll be staying at Jack's Bluff."

For a second she thought she'd heard him wrong. Only the words were still there, rumbling through her mind, prying loose old memories. "I can't go to your family's ranch."

"You have a better idea?"

None came to mind. But she couldn't become that entangled with Langston. It was too risky—for lots of reasons. She'd go with him, but only to pick up Gina. After that, she'd have to handle this on her own.

Back to Jack's Bluff. Back to the memories. Back to Langston. This was the last thing she needed now. And the only thing that made sense.

THEY LEFT TRISH'S RENTAL at the camp and took the Porsche to Jack's Bluff. Langston kept his eyes on the road and both hands on the wheel as he dealt with I-45 traffic and talked into the hands-free phone. This was his fifth call from Melvin since they'd left Dallas. The timing for being out of the office couldn't be worse.

"We'll need a full risk analysis on that project," he said as passed an eighteen-wheeler that was hogging the road.

"Do you want it done in-house?"

"No. Hire the risk analysis consultant we used on the last project. She nailed the political implications on the head."

"Angie McLaughlin. I'll give her a call today."

"And get me the latest data on Delaney's drilling project off the Louisiana coast. I'd hoped to have that up and pumping before hurricane season."

"I talked to Delaney this morning. He's blaming everyone but the Pope for the delays. Says he'll need at least two more weeks and that's only if the tropical storm in the Atlantic doesn't move into the Gulf."

"In the meantime he's running seriously over budget."

"I reminded him of that. Guess that's it for now. Oh, except that Lynnette said to tell you that the governor's PR rep called. He wants you to attend an official dinner on August twelfth with representatives from the Saudi government who'll be in Houston to discuss the global energy market."

"Have Lynnette check my calendar. If the date's open, tell her to accept the invitation." Lynnette Billings had been with the company for at least twenty years, working for his grandfather before she'd become Langston's personal secretary. He'd hate to tackle the job of running Collingsworth Oil without her.

"That's it for now," Melvin said. "Will you be in this afternoon?"

"Probably not, but you can reach me by phone if something else comes up."

"Anything I can do to help you with whatever it is you're dealing with?"

"No, it's under control." That wasn't quite the truth, but Langston had no intentions of bringing Melvin in on this. He never liked mixing business with his personal life.

Not that *personal* accurately described his relationship with Trish. She was more stranger than anything else at this point. She'd cried in his arms at the lake, but she'd retreated back into a shell of a silence since they'd been on the road.

"You seem to have a lot of responsibility with Collingsworth Oil," Trish said, speaking for the first time in the past thirty miles.

"I'm a very hands-on president."

"President of Collingsworth Oil? At your age? I'm impressed."

"It helps when your family owns the company."

"Is your grandfather still CEO?"

"He was until he had a stroke three weeks ago."

"Is he going to be okay?"

"No one seems to have a definitive answer on that. His body's mending, but his mind seems to have shut down."

"I hate to hear that. He was always so in tune with everything."

"Right up to the time of the stroke."

She shifted in her seat, turning so that she could look at him. He met her gaze for a second before turning back to the road. Her eyes were slightly swollen from her earlier tears, making her look incredibly vulnerable.

"Does your family know that you're bringing me to the ranch?"

"I explained the situation to Matt."

"And did he tell you that you were crazy to become involved in my problems?"

"It seems the word *crazy* might have been bandied about. But don't worry about Matt. He likes to give advice, but he'd have done the same in my situation."

His cell phone rang again. Celeste. Damn. He should have called her before now, but it had completely slipped his mind. He took the call. "Good morning, Celeste. I was just about to ring you."

"I tried to get you, but your line was busy."

"Taking care of business."

"When are you coming home?"

"I'm headed that way as we speak."

"Good. Shall I get dinner reservations for tonight or would you like to order in?"

"Best not to plan on me for dinner. I have to stop off at the ranch and I may be late getting into town."

"You're going to the ranch again?"

"Sorry. It can't be helped."

"Very well. I'll make other plans. So was the abduction business a scam as I suspected?"

"Quite the contrary, but Trish is okay now. I'll explain everything when I see you."

"Whenever that might be. Don't get so involved with playing hero to this woman that you forget the fund-raiser Mother is hosting for the governor on Saturday night. She'd be terribly disappointed if you weren't there."

"I wouldn't want to miss the governor." He said his goodbyes, and then glanced at Trish. She was staring straight ahead, the muscles in her face and neck showing the strain of the past few days. There was no way this had been a simple carjacking, but it wasn't a scam, either—at least not on Trish's part. The answers to all of this had to lie in that missing video.

So all they needed was the video. And all he needed was to keep the memories of his summer with Trish in the lock-and-hold position until both Trish and Gina were out of danger. Surely he could manage that.

TRISH FELT THE STRESS BUILDING as Langston stopped the Porsche in the driveway at Jack's Bluff. She'd loved the ranch from her very first visit. It had a sense of home she'd never felt in the dozens of rented apartments and houses where she'd lived with her dad.

She'd tried to re-create that same sense of warmth and love in the house where she and Gina lived in Dallas. She'd only partially succeeded. The ranch had a continuity about it that stemmed from roots stretching across several generations, and from the boisterous laughter and life that only a large family could bring to a structure of wood and brick.

"Mom!"

Trish jumped from the car the second she heard her daughter's voice. Gina was running toward her, her dark curls dancing about her head, her arms pumping at her side. She threw herself into Trish's arms and they both held on tightly.

Too soon, Gina pulled away. "Is everything okay now?"

"It's a long story."

"But you're fine, right?"

"I'm fine, sweetheart."

Trish brushed errant locks from Gina's face and let her fingers linger on her daughter's soft cheek. The scariest part of the past few days had been the fear that she might never see her daughter again or that somehow the danger would stretch to envelop Gina. She'd do anything to keep her safe, but she couldn't protect her from the fact that Selena had been murdered or that the killer was still on the loose.

Trish turned and saw several people including Langston's mother standing at the back door peering out at them. She would have known Lenora Collingsworth anywhere. The years had been very kind to her.

"Zach and I were just going horseback riding," Gina said, the excitement raising her voice an octave or two. "He's already at the stables saddling our mounts. I'm riding Candy. She's black and so beautiful. She has this white star right on her forehead."

"She sounds beautiful," Trish said, making the easy decision that the news of Selena's death could wait awhile longer.

"Do you want to come with us? There are lots of horses at Jack's Bluff."

"Not this time," Trish assured her, "but you go ahead."

Gina glanced back to the stables. "Are you sure you don't mind?"

"Not at all. Go for your ride and we'll talk when you get back."

Gina gave her quick hug, then took off in the direction of the stables as Trish followed Langston to the back door, haunted by memories of a time when she was only a few years older than Gina was now. And certain that she had to take Gina and get out of there as quickly as possible, before the secrets of her past came crashing down on all of them.

LANGSTON SAT IN THE KITCHEN with Matt and Bart. It was amazing how all their major battles ended up here around the scarred oak table and the coffeepot. And this would be a battle, though Matt had been polite and hospitable while Trish had explained the carjacking and the subsequent events. But now that their mother had taken Trish to the powder room to freshen up, Matt's irritation was as obvious as the fangs on a striking rattlesnake.

"I don't buy it," Matt said. "Why the hell would a carjacker give a random victim this mystery video?"

"Don't you listen?" Bart argued. "She says she doesn't have it." He scratched his smooth-shaven chin. "It's that Gary Packard fellow that puzzles me. I know there are crooked cops, but the whole idea of him showing up on an isolated stretch of country road just in time to save Trish's life and then breaking into her house and shop and murdering her employee is pretty far-fetched, even for Dallas."

"I know there are questions," Langston said. "I have a lot of them myself, but I honestly believe Trish is telling the truth."

Matt grunted. "Based on what—the fact that you had the hots for her sixteen years ago?"

"No, based on what I've seen of her over the past few hours. She's confused, scared and heartbroken over what happened to Selena Hernandez, but she's never shown any sign of faking the emotions. And I've seen her house. It looked like a wrecking crew had gone through it. The demolition had all the signs of someone searching for something."

Matt shook his head and refilled his coffee mug.

"You have a blind spot where Trish Cantrell's concerned. You always have."

"So what are you planning to do?" Bart asked.

"Keep her and Gina from getting killed while I find out what's going on."

"Any plans for how you're going to do that?"

"Nothing firm. I'd like Gina to stay here at the ranch. She seems to have bonded with Zach, and he has nothing better to do than keep her occupied."

"What about Trish?" Matt asked.

That was the big question, and one Langston hadn't come to terms with himself. He needed to be near her if he was going to be involved in the investigation, but he couldn't stay away from the office indefinitely.

"She can stay here, too," Bart said. "Whatever trouble she's in, we can handle it. Hell, who's going to mess with three Collingsworth brothers, four when you're around?"

"No way," Matt said. "Trish is not staying at Jack's Bluff. If Langston wants to take her on, he can take her to Houston with him."

No one had heard Lenora approach but now she stamped into the middle of the room and positioned her body directly in front of Matt. "Of all the heartless things to say, Matt Collingsworth. I know I've raised you better than that."

"You raised me to use my head for more than to hold up a Stetson. There's no valid reason to believe anything Trish Cantrell has said."

"I hate to admit it, but Matt has a point," Bart agreed.

"Are you all blind?" Lenora demanded, pausing to stare each of them down. "Did you not see her with Gina? And have you not heard the way Gina's talked

about her mother? Trish didn't willingly become
involved in anything that put her daughter in danger."

Lenora pulled herself to her full five-foot-four frame
and propped her hands on her slim hips. "Trish and Gina
will stay here at Jack's Bluff, and you will all treat them
as guests while Langston finds out what's going on."

Matt threw up his hands as if he were dealing with
a horse that wasn't worth breaking.

Langston smiled at his mother. The woman might be
wearing a dress, but she had balls.

"And who's going to keep the trouble from following them here?" Matt said, giving this one last shot.

"My sons," Lenora said. "And if you can't handle the
job, hire people who can. What good is having the resources we do if we can't help others? I suggest you talk
to Billy Mack. He has a good friend who was a Texas
Ranger." She reached in the refrigerator for a bottle of
drinking water. "I'm going to put Trish in the guest
room next to Gina's. And then, if there's no other issues
to settle here, I'm going to my office in Houston."

"Whoa," Langston said. "What office?"

"The office of the CEO, of course. I just want to look
it over and see where I'll be spending my time." And
with that she headed out the kitchen door, leaving her
sons staring with their mouths slightly agape.

Langston leaned against the counter. "Now we may
have more trouble than we can handle."

GINA THREW HERSELF ACROSS the bed in her room at the
ranch, landing on her stomach and propping herself up
on her elbows so that she could look at Trish while they

talked. Her face was glowing from the wind and sun, her eyes from the excitement of the ride.

"Zach is really cool," she said. "So is his sister, Jaime. They're twins, but they don't look alike. He has dark hair. Jaime has blond."

"I know. They're fraternal twins."

"That's what Mrs. Collingsworth said. She's neat, too. And this ranch, wow! It rocks, I mean, it's so big. We rode for an hour and never left the property. And Matt and Bart both have their own houses on the ranch, and you can't even see them from here."

"Jack's Bluff is the second-largest ranch in Texas," Trish said, making idle conversation while she considered how best to explain Selena's death and the continuing danger they were facing.

For Gina, the fear and anxiety had dissolved the moment she talked to her mother on the phone last night and knew she was with Langston and was safe. Now she had to drag her back into the mire, and this time she could offer no easy reassurances. Nor could she put it off.

The murder was all over the news. Trish had made certain the TV was turned off when Zach and Gina had returned from their ride, but it was only a matter of time before Gina would hear it for herself.

"So, how do you know the Collingsworths, Mom? I've never heard you mention them."

No reason to lie, at least not about this. "Langston and I dated one summer."

"*Oh.*" She rolled over and pulled up to a sitting position in the middle of the bed, letting her ankles dangle over the edge. "Was that before you met my father?"

"Yes."

"So why did you send me here? And why did you make it so secretive and talk about the police?"

Trish took a deep breath and dropped to the edge of the bed, finally deciding there was no way to say this except straight out. "It's complicated and I have some bad news."

Gina scooted forward until they were side by side, her mood changing in an instant.

Trish wrapped her arm about Gina's shoulders. "This is about Selena, Gina. She was murdered this morning."

Gina looked up at her, the shock and horror mirrored in her wide eyes. "No, no way! Not our Selena."

"I know how upsetting this is, but…"

"Where? Who did it?"

"She was in the shop. We don't know who did it."

Gina started to shake and Trish pulled her into her arms, holding on tightly and burying her face in Gina's mass of thick curls.

"I'm sorry, sweetheart. Really sorry."

"But who would kill her? Everybody likes Selena." Gina pulled away and looked up at Trish. "This is about the trouble you were in yesterday. It's why you sent me here to the ranch, isn't it?"

"There's a good chance it's all connected." Trish tried to explain the situation without frightening Gina any more than she already was. She gave her most of the details, but left out the part about believing that a Dallas detective might be involved.

"Why didn't you call me at the camp and tell me as soon as you'd been carjacked?"

"I didn't want to worry you."

"It worried me more when you told me to come to Jack's Bluff Ranch and then you just stopped talking."

"I was driving and hit a dead spot. I didn't get a signal again after that."

"The man who killed Selena's still out there. If he's the one who thinks you have that video, he could be looking for you."

Smart girl, her Gina, and Trish wouldn't insult her by pretending she was overreacting. "I'm aware of the danger. So is Langston. That's why he's offered to help us in any way he can."

"Will he let us stay at the ranch until they arrest the killer?"

"I'm sure he would if we decided to do that, but we have lots of options." She just hadn't figured out what they were yet.

"Then let's stay here. We'd have the killer outnumbered. There are four guys here, and they have guns, too. Shotguns and everything. There's a locked case of weapons in the den. I saw them this morning."

"Those are collector items." But Trish was certain all the Collingsworth brothers had other guns as well.

"Poor Enrico. What will he do without Selena?" A tear rolled down Gina's cheek as the sadness pushed through the shock and fear. "They were in love."

Trish pulled her daughter close. "I know, sweetheart, I know."

"I can't believe she's dead." Gina sobbed and Trish felt her own tears burning at the back of her eyes. They held on and cried softly together until the grief was interrupted by a light rapping on the door.

"Come in."

The door creaked open and Langston stepped inside. "I hate to disturb you, but I just got off the phone with an attorney. He's agreed to see you this afternoon, but we'll have to leave for Houston now. He's flying to Waco at six for a trial that starts tomorrow."

"I didn't ask you to call an attorney."

"His name's Phil Caruthers," he went on, ignoring her comment. "You may have heard of him."

Oh, she'd heard of him all right. He was the defense attorney who'd represented Senator Mohagen last year when he'd been accused of killing his wife. The senator had not only been acquitted, but had been reelected thanks to Caruthers's brilliant handling of the case.

"Even if I needed an attorney, I couldn't afford Phil Caruthers."

"You'll just be talking to him at this point, getting his advice."

Gina dabbed at her eyes with back of her hands. "Why does my mother need a lawyer?"

"Attorneys are a good buffer when you're dealing with the police."

"But the police should already be out looking for the killer."

"I'm sure they are," Langston said, "but the police will want to talk to your mother, too, and like I said, a good attorney can facilitate that. We should leave in the next ten minutes. Gina, you can stay here at the ranch. I've already talked to my brothers. They'll all three be here this afternoon, and Bart said you can go with him to move some cattle into the northwest pasture."

He was doing it again, making decisions for her as if she were incapable of making her own. "Gina, would you excuse Langston and me for a minute? We need to talk in private."

Gina looked up at her, her eyes shadowed with anxiety and sadness now instead of the excitement that had shone in them when she'd returned from the ride. "Okay, but I don't mind staying here—just as long you'll be safe."

"I'll make sure that she is," Langston promised.

Gina squeezed Trish's hand, then scooted past Langston and out the door. Trish waited until her daughter's footsteps had receded down the hall and to the staircase. She took a deep breath, hoping that her voice didn't betray how shaky and unsure she was.

"I appreciate your help, Langston, but I have to do this my way."

"Which would be?"

"I'll need to borrow a vehicle, but I'll get it back to you as soon as I can."

"The police will be looking for you. They may even suspect you've been involved in foul play as well."

"I'll call the DPD and assure them that I'm safe for now, but after that I just need to take Gina and get out of town until this is cleared up."

"You are out of town."

"Then maybe I'll get out of the country. I've always wanted to go to Australia. We could spend a couple of months there."

Langston closed the door and stepped closer, staring at her so intently she felt as if he were pushing her against the wall. "I didn't go looking for you, Trish. You pulled me into this when you sent Gina here. I'm in it now, and I can't sit back and watch you make foolish decisions that put both you and Gina in danger."

"I can handle this, Langston."

"By taking Gina and going on the run?"

"Just until the murderer is in custody or until he realizes that I don't have the video."

"The cops will be looking for you, Trish. You'll be arrested the second you try to leave the country—or before."

"I haven't done anything wrong."

"Innocent until proven guilty only works in old movies." He took her hands. She hadn't realized hers were trembling until she felt them encased in his. "I had a call from Aidan."

"Your Houston detective friend?"

Langston nodded. "He heard from his contact with the DPD that the surveillance cameras from Cottage Bouquet have been taken into the station."

"Do they show the murder?"

"The cameras were disconnected. The perpetrator obviously knew where they were and how to avoid them, but they have several shots of Buck Rivers entering and leaving the boutique over the past two weeks. In at least two of them, he's talking to Selena."

"There must be a mistake."

"I wouldn't count on it."

"I knew he looked familiar, but I don't remember seeing him in the shop or waiting on him."

"I believe you, but the fact that he was in and out of the shop indicates that it wasn't a random carjacking. He chose you for a reason."

Which meant the rest of the police, like Gary Packard, would suspect that she and Buck Rivers were somehow in cahoots. They might even think she was behind Selena's murder.

"Give me a chance, Trish. Let me help—for old time's sake."

For old time's sake. Only he had no idea how long the heartbreak of walking away from him had lasted. He had no idea how many lies lay between them.

"For Gina's sake. My brothers will be at the ranch at all times, and they'll make sure no stranger comes near her."

For Gina's sake. The one argument she couldn't fight. "Okay, Langston. I'll talk to Caruthers. I'll give you a decision about whether we stay or go after that."

"Once you've talked to him, you'll realize that staying with me is your best option."

That remained to be seen.

Chapter Six

Phil Caruthers's office was on Main Street in downtown Houston, a few blocks from the theater district. The building was modern, steel and so much glass that it shimmered in the bright afternoon sun. Had Trish had any doubt of the attorney's success, it would have vanished when she stepped off the elevator on the twenty-seventh floor and entered the double glass doors of the reception area.

With the pale gray carpet, deep red walls and crystal chandelier, it looked like the lobby of a fashionable, European hotel. Two plush sofas in black leather claimed the center of the room, and the chairs scattered about the area were upholstered in a muted pale gray and deep red plaid. A huge vase of fresh flowers sat on a round table in the center of the room.

There was no desk or window to go to for service, but within seconds after their arrival, a very attractive and smartly dressed woman who appeared to be in her mid-thirties opened a door and welcomed them. Trish was thankful she'd at least changed into the pair of clean jeans and white blouse that Becky had insisted on lending her.

"I'm Jerri Conti, Mr. Caruthers' assistant, and you must be Langston Collingsworth," the woman said, extending a perfectly manicured hand and flashing a seductive smile.

"Yes, and this is Trish Cantrell."

Her smile remained, but it lost some of its sparkle when it moved from Langston to Trish. Even at nineteen, Langston had garnered more than his share of attention from females. But now sophistication and power had added charisma to his arsenal, and Trish was certain that he attracted female attention wherever he went. From what she'd heard of his phone conversations, he probably also had a significant other.

"Mr. Caruthers will be with you in a few minutes. Can I get you something while you wait? A soft drink? Water? Coffee?"

"Coffee sounds good," Trish answered, though she wasn't sure added caffeine would be good for her jumpy nerves.

"Nothing for me," Langston said.

Phil Caruthers made his appearance before the arrival of the coffee. He was slightly past middle-aged, balding, short and about thirty pounds overweight—most of that riding over his belt. The belt was expensive. So was the suit and the crocodile western boots.

"You made good time," he said. "Traffic can be awful this time of the day." He strode into the room with them, but unlike the secretary, he gave only a passing glance to Langston before focusing all his attention on Trish. There was, however, nothing seductive in his look.

"I've just been learning all about you on the news. Sounds like you got trouble, Ms. Cantrell."

"I most definitely have trouble," she agreed, "though I don't know what you heard."

"Police all over the state are looking for you. Why don't you come on back to the office? I don't have long, but I'd like to hear your version of the situation before we decide how to handle the police. Like I told Langston on the phone, once they know you're alive and well, they'll expect you to come in for questioning. If you refuse, they'll get a warrant for your arrest."

"How can they issue a warrant for my arrest? I'm not accused of anything."

"They'll still say you're a person of interest. It's how the game is played—at least if we play by their rules. Which we won't. You have a right to protection, and you can be damn sure they won't provide it."

He turned and they followed him to his office. Within ten minutes, she'd told him and the tape recorder on his desk all she knew. If anything, retelling the story to the attorney made the situation seem even more bizarre. She sensed that Caruthers found it so as well.

He made a few notes on a legal pad on his desk, and then looked up. "Do you think it's possible that Buck Rivers had been coming to the shop to visit with Selena?"

Oddly, that possibility hadn't even occurred to Trish. "I'm pretty sure she didn't know him. She'd never mentioned him, and we talked about everything."

"And you hadn't noticed anything amiss at the shop?"

"I'm not sure what you mean."

"Shoplifting? Money missing from the register? Mistakes in the books?"

"No. Nothing like that." She wasn't sure what he was

getting at, but Selena would never steal from her. She was certain of that.

"I'll do all the talking to the police," the attorney said, as if his taking her case were a done deal, although there had been no mention of price. "I'll assure them you are safe but that you are obviously worried about you and your daughter's safety. If they want to talk to you, they'll have to do it when I can be present."

"What if they issue a warrant for my arrest?"

"They won't, at least not based on the information they have now, not when we're agreeing for you to answer their questions. One thing, though, Mrs. Cantrell, I don't want any surprises. I can handle the case, but I need to know everything up front."

"I've told you everything I know. I'm not guilty of any wrongdoing."

"I'm not concerned about your guilt. That's for the jury to worry about and I don't expect this to go that far. My job is to see that the police play by the rules and that your rights aren't compromised in any way. I just don't want to be blindsided when I'm dealing with the DPD. Now, is there anything in your past that will throw up a red flag?"

"I don't know what you mean," she said, knowing pretty much everything in her past would throw up red flags if it all came to light.

"Do you have a criminal record?"

"No, not even a parking ticket." Not under the name of Trish Cantrell.

"What about your daughter's father?"

"What about him?"

"Could he be behind this in any way, have any reason to want to get back at you or to have you killed?"

"No. James Albee was killed in a car wreck in London before Gina was born. We were never married." At least those statements were fact.

"Okay, I'll get in touch with the police and then get back to you. In the meantime, Langston, it's up to you to make good on your word to keep Trish and her daughter safe, and the best way to do that is not to let anyone know she's with you."

Trish sat up straighter in her chair. "Langston isn't responsible for me."

"No, but he's offered his help, and I suggest you take it. Oh, and one more thing, I wouldn't mention to anyone else that you think the detective could be guilty of criminal behavior. We'll use it if and when the time comes—but keep it to yourself for now."

They said their goodbyes with still no mention of fees. She'd pay Langston back in full. It might take years, but she'd do it.

Five minutes later, they were in the car and in horrendous traffic. Langston gunned the engine, making it through the yellow light just before it flashed red. "I need to pick up some things at my condo and then stop off at the office before we head back to the ranch. I hope you don't mind."

"Of course, I don't mind." A blatant lie. She minded a lot. The last place she wanted to go was to Collingsworth Oil. Even more than the ranch, it would hold the reminders of their falling in love. Indiscreet glances at the water fountain. Shared kisses in the janitorial closet.

She forced the heated memories from her thoughts,

replacing them with the nightmare of the present, then called Gina just to make sure her daughter was okay. She was still on the line with her when Langston pulled in front of a high-rise condominium and tossed his keys to a valet.

"This is home," he said.

The valet opened her door and she stepped out. Langston led her past the uniformed doorman to a glass elevator that offered a fantastic view of the interior courtyard below as they ascended to the penthouse level.

"You actually live in this building?"

"For now. I travel a lot on company business, so it suits me better than a house."

From Jack's Bluff to the penthouse. It was less than two hours away, but it felt like a different world, and Trish had difficulty imagining how a man who fit in so well at the ranch could also fit in this world. Yet he moved between them effortlessly.

He unlocked the door and waited for her to enter first. His hand was at the small of her back, and his breath close to her ear when she heard the woman's voice.

"Is that you, Lang?"

"It's me. And a guest."

A striking young woman dressed in an exquisite white sundress stepped from the hallway into the massive living room. She rushed over and greeted Langston with a kiss on the mouth before turning to Trish.

"I don't believe we've met," she said, locking her arm with Langston's.

"This is Trish Cantrell," Langston said. "And Trish, this is Celeste Breemer, my fiancée."

The news that Langston was engaged shouldn't have come as such a surprise and definitely shouldn't have caused the disappointment that was knotting inside her.

Forcing a smile and extending a hand, she struggled to hide her emotions. "I'm pleased to meet you. I only wish it were under happier circumstances." But under other circumstances, she wouldn't have been meeting her at all. Trish had no place in Langston's life. She could tell by the stiffness in the handshake that Celeste felt the same.

"Did you come to pick up your daughter?" Celeste asked. "I understand she spent the night at Jack's Bluff."

"Actually, both Trish and Gina are going to be staying at the ranch for a while," Langston said, "but that's for your ears only. Until we're sure exactly what's going on, it's better than no one knows where to find her."

"I see. I guess that means the circumstances haven't improved."

"Unfortunately not," Trish said, "but I'm hopeful they will soon."

She wondered how much Celeste knew of the situation or of her past relationship to Langston. But then if they were engaged, there shouldn't be secrets between them.

"If you two will excuse me for a minute, I need to pack a few things," Langston said. "Would you mind fixing a drink for Trish? With the day she's had, something strong is in order."

Celeste stepped between him and the door to the hall. "Are you planning to be away overnight?"

"I have to drive Trish back to the ranch, and I thought I'd just stay the night instead of driving back. This is the night you're going to the theater with your mother, or do I have the wrong date for that?"

"We're going to the ballet," she corrected him. "You were invited."

"Men in tights make me nervous," he said, though he sounded more preoccupied than teasing. He left them standing together in the middle of the room.

Celeste tossed her head so that her silky blond hair danced about her bare shoulders and stared after him until he disappeared in the hall of the lavish suite. "Langston said you're an old friend of the Collingsworths."

Then he hadn't been totally truthful. "That's right. I've known them for years."

"Are you from Colts Run Cross?"

"No. I worked for Collingsworth Oil years ago. I was a college student and Langston's family were gracious enough to take me under their wing."

"Yes, they are the type to take in strangers. The bar's fully stocked," she said, motioning to a huge wet bar in the back right corner of the room. "Help yourself. I need to talk with Lang before he goes rushing off again. He's extremely busy these days. I can't imagine how he's found time to add your problems to his agenda."

Nor did Trish, but she resented Celeste's tone. It wasn't as if she'd begged for Langston's help. She went to the bar and checked the offerings. She seldom drank hard liquor, but Langston was right. A real drink seemed called for now.

She ran her fingers over the tops of several bottles, scanning the labels. She decided on a vodka martini, then changed her mind as she started to pour. She'd barely eaten all day, and strong liquor on an empty stomach would make her dizzy if not downright sick.

More important, it would dull her senses when she needed them at their strongest. She reeled again at the thought of Selena dying at the hands of a brutal killer. Like Celeste, Selena had been planning her wedding, preparing for a life with the man she loved. Two bullets to the head had wiped all that away in a heartbeat.

Settling on a cold beer from the under-counter refrigerator, Trish slipped her hand into her pocket, pulled out her cell phone and tried Enrico's number again. This time he answered, and the grief in his voice tore right through Trish's control. She brushed a cocktail napkin across her wet eyes.

"I'm so sorry, Enrico. So sorry."

"Yeah."

His voice cracked on the meaningless response, and she knew he was choking on his own tears.

"I'm okay," he said, though he obviously wasn't. "This is just so hard."

"Is someone with you?"

"My sister. The cops just left."

"Do they have any leads on the killer?"

"Not that they admitted. Most of their questions were about you and that carjacker who was killed. They kept asking if I knew him."

"*I* didn't even know him."

"I told them that. I don't think they believed me. Where are you?"

"I'm with a friend."

"Here in Dallas?"

"No, but I'm safe. So is Gina."

"I'm glad you called," he said. "I'm having Selena's body sent home to her family in Brownsville as soon as the police complete the autopsy and release it. After that, I'm driving down there to be with them. I don't know when I'll be back. I may just head on down into Mexico and stay there awhile."

"She loved you, Enrico, remember that. And take care."

"Why? Why the hell take care now?" His voice broke again.

Trish was glad his sister was with him, though she knew it wouldn't help all that much. Nothing could really help when you lost someone you loved. She knew that all too well.

Celeste was all gracefulness and smiles when she came back into the room with Langston. Apparently whatever had conspired between them in the bedroom had assuaged her irritation. Langston still looked distracted and remained quiet as he and Trish took the elevator to the ground floor. The car was waiting.

"One more stop to pick up some paperwork that needs my attention tonight, and we'll head back to the ranch."

"I appreciate all you've done, Langston, but you don't have to keep rearranging your life for me. I know how busy you are. I can rent a car and drive back to the ranch."

He threw on the brakes and skidded to a stop at the light that had just turned red. "How long are you going to keep this up?"

"Excuse me!"

"Every time I turn around you're pushing me out of your life. Can't you just gracefully accept help from someone when they volunteer it?"

"Yes, but…"

"No buts. I don't know what the hell you've stumbled into, but you're dealing with a madman who thinks nothing of blowing off a woman's head before breakfast. I don't know if the psycho is a cop or not, but I can tell you that if he thinks you have something he wants, he didn't just throw up his hands and give up because you left Dallas."

Cars started honking the second the light turned green, and Langston revved the engine and sped through the intersection. Trish was too stunned to respond to his outburst, but Langston had made his point. She did have a difficult time accepting help, especially from him.

YEARS OF STRUGGLING TO FORGET Trish had ever been part of his life proved totally useless as Langston led the way to his office at the end of the hall on the eighteenth floor of one of the city's oldest and most stately skyscrapers. Collingsworth Oil was where they'd met. It was only natural that being here with her would bring that all back to mind.

He wondered if it were the same for her but didn't dare ask. It would only open for discussion a topic that had nowhere to go. The past was over, and there were more than enough problems in the present to claim his attention.

It was nearly six, but most of the offices in the executive wing were still occupied. He waved greetings where doors were open, but didn't stop to chat and didn't slow his pace until he passed Jeremiah's office.

The door was closed, and he wondered if his mother were still there or had just taken a precursory tour of her new digs as she'd indicated. He knocked, but there was no answer, so he continued to his own office, keenly

aware of Trish's footfalls blending with his own, hating
the unexpected arousal when her arm accidentally
brushed his.

He opened the door to his outer office and stood
back so that Trish could precede him into the room.

"Nice," she said. "A tad roomier than the cubicle I
had."

The cubicle right next to his. The memories claimed
his mind again. He'd complained at first, thought the
grandson of the owner should have had more status
than the rest of the summer interns. Jeremiah had
squashed that suggestion in about two seconds flat, and
Langston had seriously considered telling him just what
he could do with his intern program. But that was before
he'd met his cubicle neighbor.

He shook his head, disgusted with himself. He had
to stop thinking like the schoolboy he'd been then.

Trish stopped at the mahogany desk that had been
neatly cleared and readied for the next morning, the way
Lynnette always left it. She glanced at the framed photograph on the back edge, then leaned over to study the
image more closely. "She looks familiar. Is the picture
of someone I should know?"

"That's Lynnette's granddaughter. She's an Olympic
medalist in ice skating. You may have seen her compete.
If Lynnette were here, she'd tell you every detail of her
feats and how she would have won gold were it not for
one biased judge."

"I take it Lynnette is your secretary?"

He nodded. "And totally indispensable." He unlocked
the door to his private space and hurried to the leather-
topped desk, expecting to find the files he'd asked

Lynnette to leave out. There was no sign of them. Strange, since he'd talked to her just before five, and she'd assured him the paperwork from the Saudi deal had arrived and was waiting for his perusal.

"Is something wrong?" Trish asked.

"The paperwork I stopped by for isn't here." He scanned his in-box and the notes Lynnette had left, then punched Lynnette's number into the cell phone.

He got nothing but the recorded instructions for leaving a message. "Lynnette, it's Langston. I've checked my desk for the ILC proposal, but…"

"I have it right here."

He turned as Melvin marched into the room and dropped the stapled pages onto his desk. "Excuse the call, Lynnette. Melvin's the culprit."

"I noticed it on your desk when I brought over the Gallager project report," Melvin said. "I took the liberty of giving it a once-over since I didn't know when you'd be in."

"How'd it look?"

"Not ready for prime time. I'd say you have months of negotiation ahead of you before they'll meet your terms unless you convince them up front that we aren't going to bend. I have that conference in Saudi next week. I could swing by and do a face-to-face with them then."

Langston slid the proposal into his briefcase. "We'll talk about it next week."

Melvin stood by the desk, staring at Trish admiringly and waiting for an introduction. Melvin was tanned and blond and looked more like a tennis pro than an executive. Truth was, he wouldn't have worked his way up so fast in Collingsworth Oil if Jeremiah hadn't taken him on as one of the chosen few. Once Jeremiah took a shine to you, you were in.

In Melvin's case, it had paid off. He was bright, energetic and competitive. He overstepped his bounds at times, but even Langston had trouble believing the guy was only thirty years old or that he'd just started in the oil business two years ago. He was the most competent VP they'd ever had in new drilling explorations.

Langston made the introductions, knowing that even though Melvin was aware of the situation—it was all over the news—he wouldn't bring it up or press Trish for information. He was far too savvy for that.

"Your mother was in today," Melvin said as the three of them walked out of the office. "She caused quite a stir. Everyone's wondering if she'll actually play a role in running the show."

"Assure them that she won't."

"Are you sure of that?"

"She may offer some input into ranch operations, but she knows nothing about the oil business. She'll take one look at the legalities and complicated contracts and head for a meeting of one of her many charities. My mother's smart, but this isn't her thing."

"That's not the impression I got. She had me answering questions about personnel and business policies for an hour this afternoon."

Langston groaned. He didn't need this, especially not now. "Pray Jeremiah gets well soon."

Melvin left them at the elevator, and they rode down alone. Trish stood several feet away from him, watching the numbers as they descended. She reminded him of a cat trapped in a room with a mean dog, just warily waiting for the moment the door would open and she could cut and run.

Cut and run. That's pretty much what she'd done before. One minute they were making love; the next she was gone.

But he wasn't nineteen and in heat now, and the repercussions of her running could cost her life. That's why he couldn't let her take off until this was settled and Selena's killer was behind bars. He'd see that it happened, but to do that he needed straight and complete facts, not suppositions and blind trust.

That's why he'd made the call from his apartment and why Clay Markham, reputably one of the best private detectives in Houston, was already at work digging up every jot of info available on Buck Rivers and Gary Packard. Langston didn't know what he was looking for at this juncture, but hopefully he'd know when he heard it.

"If you're hungry, we can stop somewhere and grab a bite," he said. "If not, we can join the family for dinner at the ranch. Juanita always prepares for at least twice the number that show up at the table."

"Let's join the family," she said. "I don't want to leave Gina any longer than I have to."

"Then back to Jack's Bluff it is."

And to another night under the same roof as Trish Cantrell. The memories started kicking around in his mind like a bucking bronc who'd just shoved his way out of the gate. The hardest part of this whole situation might be keeping them under control, but losing control could result in the *second* biggest mistake of his life.

Falling for her originally held first place in the mistake category. Nothing else had ever come close.

Chapter Seven

Lenora's low heels clicked along the tiled floor in the hospital's corridor as she made the familiar trek to Jeremiah's room. She and Randolph had moved into the big house with Jeremiah and Corrine the year they'd gotten married. She'd been barely twenty at the time and while she'd loved her new mother-in-law on sight, it had taken her several years to feel any fondness for Jeremiah.

She'd thought he drank too much, talked too loudly and was far too vocal and dogmatic about his politics, his sports and any other topic that caught his interest. He'd grown on her slowly, but it wasn't until Corrine was diagnosed with cancer that Trish finally realized that his antagonizing bluntness was a mere facade to keep her or anyone else from seeing what a softy he really was, especially when it came to his devotion to his family.

Corrine had died thirty-one years ago, less than a week after Lenora gave birth to Becky. Becky was the first girl born into the family in two generations, and Lenora was convinced that her mother-in-law had held onto life tenaciously even after her body had given up, just so that she could hold her precious granddaughter before she died.

They'd all been devastated at Corrine's death, especially Jeremiah, who'd slipped into a depression that lasted almost a year. Lenora had feared the same kind of reaction from him ten years later when the helicopter Randolph had been flying for the Air National Guard had crashed while on routine maneuvers, killing Randolph and three others.

But that time, she'd been the one dragged under by grief. Jeremiah had pitched in and helped her take care of her six children; the youngest, Zach and Jaime, were only four years old at the time. Jeremiah had been there for Corrine and for Lenora when they had needed him most, and now she'd be here for him—even if he didn't know it.

"I think he's looking for you," one of the young nurses said when Lenora passed their station. "You're later than usual."

"I had some business to take care of in town. What makes you think he's noticed?"

"He's more restless than usual, and he's been staring at the door for the past half hour."

"Has there been any change since morning?"

"He hasn't tried to communicate, but he helped feed himself tonight, and he really lit up when your daughter Jaime stopped in this afternoon. I'm pretty sure he recognized her, though he wouldn't look at her when she had to go."

So Jaime had been to see her grandfather. Lenora knew all the others had been in several times, but it surprised her a little that Jaime had visited. It was one of the more responsible things she'd done of late. Her daughter had a good heart and a great mind. She just liked to keep them under wraps.

Lenora slipped into Jeremiah's room quietly. He was facing the door just as the nurse had said, but he showed no sign that he recognized her. The blankness of his expression and the vacant stare added a layer of pressure to her heart and took the spring from her step.

She walked to the side of his bed and put her hand on his thin one. "Good evening, Jeremiah. I know I'm running late, but in a way, that's your fault for naming me CEO. I went down to the office today and spent some time getting the feel of the place."

She pulled a chair close to the bed and perched on the front edge of it, still close enough to keep her hand on his. He was in there somewhere, and even the doctor had said that touch and familiar voices were as good a medicine at this point as anything he could prescribe.

"The office is a busy place, far too hectic for me. I like your secretary, though. Martha's very efficient and has a great smile. I like Langston's secretary, too. He wasn't in today, and that brings me to the real excitement at the ranch."

Jeremiah stirred, but only to reach for the glass of water on his bedside table. Lenora got it for him and held the straw to his lips. He took a couple of sips, then turned away. Lenora slipped out of her shoes and stretched her toes.

"Do you remember a girl that Langston dated once named Trish Edwards?"

Jeremiah turned his head toward her.

"Trish Edwards," she said again, wondering if that was what had triggered his movement.

But he'd checked out again—if indeed he'd ever checked in. She wished he could talk. She needed advice.

She'd insisted that Trish and Gina stay at the ranch. Now she was having serious second thoughts. After all, how much could she really tell by watching one encounter between Trish and Gina?

Lenora stayed with Jeremiah awhile longer, but now she was as unaware of him as he was of her. Her thoughts were all on the two virtual strangers that she'd invited into her home. It was the hospitable thing to do, but Lenora couldn't help but wonder if she'd made a perilous mistake.

A LIGHT MIST WAS FALLING WHEN the young man in his neatly pressed twill trousers and light blue polo shirt drove away from the handicapped children's camp just south of Dallas. It was amazing how helpful people could be when he flashed a fake police ID he'd printed online that morning, especially with the rumor of possible foul play to Gina's mother the top story on every Texas newscast. Honest people were so gullible.

He'd talked to the counselor who'd driven Gina to catch a Greyhound bus home. The counselor was horrified that Gina might have also met with foul play. She was such a charming and smart girl, the counselor had kept repeating, as if being nice was a magical shield to ward off danger.

He hit a slick spot and his tires spun, throwing mud everywhere, including all over his freshly washed car. He spat out a stream of curses and flicked on the radio to see if the DPD had located Trish or her daughter yet. He hoped not. This would be a lot easier if he found them first. A quick look at the Greyhound tickets sales ledger and a nice chat with a couple of drivers and he'd know exactly where Gina had gone that day. One thing was certain. She hadn't gone home.

From what he'd heard, Trish was no novice at disappearing without a trace. But her time was up.

The truth was that nice people got hit with disaster all the time. Bang, bang. Good-bye.

Nothing personal, at least not for him. He was just earning a check.

LANGSTON FINISHED HIS conversation with Phil Caruthers and followed the sound of voices to the back porch. Just once he'd like to get a reassuring call from someone regarding Trish's predicament. This wasn't it. He'd have to pass the news on to Trish, but he'd wait until he could talk to her alone.

Strange thing about Jack's Bluff Ranch. No matter how much trouble was brewing in Langston's life, a visit to the ranch usually made him feel as if all was right with the world. That was definitely not the case tonight. He couldn't think of anything beyond the fact that a killer could be carrying around a bullet with Trish's name on it. And judging by the tension at dinner tonight, everyone else must be having the same problem.

Lenora and Trish were having after-dinner coffee now, decaffeinated with a splash of chocolate liqueur. His mother swore it was better than any sleeping pill. Gina was reading a fanzine, no doubt courtesy of Jaime, and Matt was having a scotch on the rocks. The rest of the family had wandered off to their own quarters.

Gina dropped the magazine she'd been looking at to the floor near the beanbag chair that she'd draped herself over. "I wish I could call my friend Janie and tell her where I am."

"No phone calls," Trish said. "Not until I say it's okay."

Trish left the sofa and joined Gina in the oversize beanbag. Snuggled together that way, Trish looked barely older than Gina. A knot swelled in Langston's throat. He swallowed hard and ignored it.

Trish slipped an arm around Gina's shoulders. "It won't be much longer, sweetheart. The killer will be in jail before you know it, and we'll be back in Dallas."

"I can't believe Selena was killed over some stupid video," Gina said. "What do you think is on it? It couldn't be us, could it?"

"No, I'm sure it's all a mistake," Trish assured her, though Langston doubted she believed that. "I think the carjacker and the killer had me mixed up with someone else."

"Well, it's still scary," Gina said, sticking to her guns. "What if the killer finds out we're here and shows up at the ranch?"

Langston perched on the arm of the sofa near her. "He's not going to find out. But if he shows up here, then we'll save the sheriff the trouble of finding him. My brothers or I will take him in."

"But what if you're not here or no one sees him? What will keep him from just walking up like I did the other day?"

"That won't happen. Every man on the ranch is on

the lookout. And tomorrow there will be more men. I'm hiring a security detail to make sure that no strangers come sneaking about the ranch."

Lenora planted her feet and stopped the creaking of her rocker. "I haven't heard about a security detail."

"I discussed it with Billy Mack while you guys were freshening up for dinner. He contacted his Texas Ranger friend and I'm meeting with him tomorrow morning here at the ranch."

"You might have mentioned it to Bart and me first," Matt said.

Langston shoved his hands into his pockets and worked at keeping his cool. He made decisions affecting multi-million-dollar proposals all day without consulting with anyone, but Matt was right. The ranch was their domain. "Do you have a problem with it?"

"Not off hand," Matt said, "but I don't think it's needed. The Collingsworths have been protecting their own women and land for generations. I can't see why this is any different."

"We don't know what we're dealing with," Langston said, not wanting to blurt out in front of Gina that they were dealing with a lunatic with a nervous gun hand and no conscience. "I figure it's always better to be prepared."

"I must say I agree with Langston," Lenora said. "It's not as if we're living in the days of the Wild West. It makes sense to hire professionals when extra security is needed, though I hope it won't come to that." She resumed her rocking. "But I'm with Gina. I'll be glad when this is over."

"We all will," Langston assured her.

Trish pushed herself out of the beanbag chair and to a standing position. "We've put you out too much," she said, her gaze fixed on Lenora. "Gina and I can make other arrangements."

Langston's blood pressure shot up like an explosive. "That's already been settled."

"Of course you won't make other arrangements," Lenora said, backing him, but without his authoritarian tone. "You and Gina will stay here as long as needed, and Langston will see that you're safe. Besides, there's no reason to think you can be tracked to the ranch."

"But…"

Whatever protest Trish was about to utter was interrupted by Jaime's arrival. She swirled to the middle of the room with her usual flair. "Can someone help me with this zipper? It's stuck."

Gina jumped up to help, apparently ready for a break in the discussion. She worked diligently until she got the bright yellow sundress zipped and in place.

"Cool dress," Gina said.

"Thanks."

"Where are you off to tonight?" Lenora asked.

"Just out with Garth. He should be here any minute."

"Out where?"

"I don't know. We might catch a movie, or go to Cutter's for some two-steppin'."

"Be careful."

"I'm twenty-five, Mom. You don't have to say that every time I walk out the door."

"Be extra careful," Langston and Bart both added together.

"Relax, guys. I'll be with Garth. He's tough. And I'm

definitely not going to stay around here with you deadbeats."

The doorbell rang. "That's Garth," Jaime said. "Later, posse."

"My mom always tells me to be careful when I go out, too," Gina told Lenora.

"Your mother wasn't even as old as Jaime is now the last time she was here on the ranch," Lenora said. "In fact she was closer to your age. How old were you, Trish?"

"Nineteen."

"She liked riding horses just like you do. She rode that sorrel mare that Randolph had bought me. Paddy. Such a spirited beauty. Do you remember her, Trish?"

"I do." Her voice was tentative, and it seemed to linger like the echoes of the past that haunted Langston's mind.

"The two of them would go off for hours, and they'd come back laughing, their faces glowing from the wind and sun just as you did."

"Do you have any pictures of her back then? I've never even seen one snapshot of her before she was my mom."

"Not that I know of, though there may be some photos of Langston and Trish in one of the old albums. I know she was here for Jaime and Zach's birthday that year. She helped me blow up balloons for the party."

Langston's insides jerked. "I need some air," he said. "I'm going for a walk."

Gina jumped to attention. "Can I go with you?"

He didn't need Trish's daughter bouncing along beside him. She was too damn much like her mother with her dark curly hair and her big, expressive eyes. Even her voice was similar. Not her fault, he reminded himself.

"Sure," he said. "But spray on some insect repellent. The mosquitoes around here make vampires look like a safe date."

TRISH STEPPED FROM THE SHOWER and took one of the thick blue towels from the rod. She wrapped it around her, sarong-style, then took another and used it to dry her hair, bending so that the dripping strands fell in front of her face. Dry enough, she decided and exchanged the towel for the new toothbrush Lenora had laid out for her along with the guest shampoo and other hygiene products.

When her mouth was minty clean, she took a good look at her face in the mirror. Her skin was smooth and the few wrinkles around her eyes were hardly noticeable at all unless she searched for them the way she was doing now.

She stepped back and let the towel that had been wrapped around her waist drop to the floor. Her figure was still good, too. Nothing but a few stretch marks from the pregnancy and perhaps a bit of sag to the breasts to mark the differences between now and the last time she'd been at Jack's Bluff.

But even then she'd known what it felt like to live in the shadows, to make friends cautiously, to keep secrets locked away so tightly that she barely allowed herself to think of them. But she hadn't known what it was like to look into the face of her child who meant more to her than life itself, and know that just by bringing her into the world, she'd brought her into a web of danger.

She wrapped the towel around her again, peeked out the bathroom door to make certain the hallway was empty, then hurried the few steps to her bedroom. The bed was turned down and ready. Unfortunately, she either had to go to Lenora or Becky and ask to borrow pajamas or she'd have to sleep naked. As tired as she was, the latter seemed preferable. She didn't know why she hadn't thought to stop somewhere on the way and purchase a few changes of clothes.

She was about to drop to the bed when there was a tap at the door. Gina must be back from her walk with Langston. She opened the door, then grabbed the towel and pulled it tighter, her fingers fumbling at the simple task.

"Langston. I thought you were Gina. I mean…" Her face burned, and when he stepped inside awareness zinged along her nerves. "I'm not dressed." Stupid. Of course he could see that.

"I thought you might need this," he said, tossing her one of his white T-shirts. "Not that you have to…"

They were both stumbling over their words, the meeting becoming much more complicated than it should have been, considering the fact that she was completely covered by the towel.

"If you give me the clothes you were wearing at the camp, I'll wash them for you."

"You can't do my laundry."

"It's a matter of punching a button and pouring in some detergent. I'm pretty sure I can handle it."

"No, I meant…" Meant that she couldn't hand him her bra and panties, especially these panties. They were the ones she wore around the house. Granny panties. Celeste probably didn't even own a pair like that.

What was she thinking? Her panties didn't matter.

She was here because someone wanted her dead. "I'd appreciate that," she said. "Otherwise I'll be meeting the security team in dirty clothes in the morning."

"Not necessarily. Becky's about your size, and she said to tell you you're welcome to raid her closet."

"I may take her up on that." She bent to pick up the clothes, and the towel slipped. She dropped the jeans and grabbed for the edge of the towel again as one nipple peeked out. The burn to her cheeks became excruciating.

Langston picked up the pile of dirty clothes. "It shouldn't be this awkward between us, Trish."

She swallowed around a burning knot in her throat. "I know. It's just that it's been a hard few days for me, especially today."

"It's got to be rough losing a friend in such a senseless murder."

"If possible, it makes it even harder knowing I was the one the killer really wanted."

"You don't know that."

"How can you say that? I was the one who was abducted at gunpoint, received a threatening phone call and had my house broken into."

"But Selena was the one who'd had previous contact with Buck Rivers. You don't really know how well she knew him."

"She wasn't physically involved with him in any way. I know that. You'd know it, too, if you knew Selena."

"Sometimes we see what we want to see in a friend."

"That's not the case with Selena."

He nodded, but she knew he wasn't convinced. Still,

the embarrassment had passed. The discussion of murder had a way of re-setting priorities.

"The call I got tonight was from Phil Caruthers," Langston said. "He's talked to the DPD."

"Why didn't you tell me earlier?"

"I didn't want to discuss it in front of Gina. She's frightened enough as it is."

Trish dropped to the edge of the bed, one hand securing the towel. "What did he say? Do I have to go in for questioning?"

"The day after tomorrow. Caruthers will meet us in Dallas."

"Did he tell them that I'm here with you?"

"No. He told them you were in hiding for your own protection and that he'd bring you in for questioning. In the process, he let slip a few miscues that hopefully convinced them you're in the West Texas area, just in case Gary Packard actually is in involved with this."

"Do they have any leads?"

"None that they're admitting. But there is something you should know."

"More bad news. I can see it your eyes."

"Gary Packard is the lead detective in the investigation."

Her insides quaked and she bit back a scream of frustration. "Where does that leave me? I'm sure the detective will be impressed when I accuse him of threatening me over some mystery video and breaking in my house. He might even be the monster who killed Selena. What then? Is he going to arrest himself?"

Her voice was rising. She was losing it, but this was just too prosperous for words. "What did Caruthers say?"

"He says he'd like to face Packard in the interrogation session. He can tell a lot about a man by the way he lies."

"Then he believes I was right, that the detective did break into my house."

"He believes that you're convinced it was Packard."

That wasn't exactly the same thing, but it would have to do for now. "What about you, Langston?" She looked up and met his eyes. They were dark and piercing, but she couldn't read them. "With all the breaking news, do you still believe in me?"

"I wouldn't be standing here if I didn't."

But he was here, much too close, and all of a sudden she ached to fit herself into his strong arms. She absolutely couldn't let him know that she was having those kinds of thoughts.

"We'll talk more in the morning," Langston said. "You need to get some rest."

His voice was husky. She only managed a nod and held her shaky breath as he crossed the room and left. Her emotions were too raw to deal with Langston. Her heart, too fragile. The costs of falling for him again, much too high.

Chapter Eight

Ron Durham, or Bull as he was affectionately known by his fellow Texas Rangers before his retirement, arrived at Jack's Bluff before breakfast on Wednesday morning. He met with the Collingsworth men and Trish and Lenora in the dining room for slightly over an hour. Both Jaime and Gina were still sleeping and Becky was in her room packing for a noon flight to visit an old girlfriend in San Diego.

Not only was the security expert ruggedly handsome and incredibly virile but he knew his stuff, at least it sounded that way to Trish. By the time he left, she was sure no unauthorized visitors would get near the house or the stables.

While it was impossible to guard the entire ranch, he had a plan for that, too. The women were not to go riding on the more secluded areas of the ranch without having a male with them, either one of his four men or one of the Collingsworth brothers—all excellent marksmen.

Neither Gina nor Trish was to leave the ranch alone, but as there was no logical reason to suspect anyone else of being in danger, only reasonable caution was advised for Lenora and Jaime. They were to keep their car doors locked at all times, avoid unpopulated areas and check in with Bull whenever they changed location or if they spotted anything suspicious.

The scope of the operation was mind-boggling to Trish, but Langston made it all seem like routine precautionary procedures. Wealth and power made everything simple.

Bull had stayed for a breakfast of *migas*, a spicy concoction of bits of corn tortillas fried crispy and tangled with eggs, chorizo, cheese and chilies—at least that was Juanita's version. It was possibly the best breakfast Trish had ever eaten in her life, and in spite of the situation, she ate as if ravenous.

The house was quiet again now, except for the kitchen where Juanita was chopping vegetables for a stew. Trish had offered her help, but Juanita had shooed her off. Left with nothing to occupy her but worrisome thoughts, Trish meandered through the downstairs rooms of the spacious old house, pausing in the den to examine the host of framed pictures on the oak bookshelves.

She lingered over one of Langston when he must have been no older than Gina was now. He was swinging across the swimming hole on a rope that hung from the branch of the ancient oak tree that grew near the bank. He was a lot scrawnier in the picture than he'd been when she'd met him. His hair was the same, thick and dark and flying in every direction.

His hair didn't fly now. It was cut to perfection, short, businesslike, always in place. She wondered if Celeste had ever seen it wild and unruly after a jump into the old swimming hole, wondered if she'd ever heard that Tarzan yell of his when he was flying on his rope or seen him grin in that mischievous way he'd done at nineteen when he was about to pick Trish up and throw her into the water, clothes and all.

"Mom, what are you doing in here by yourself? I've been looking for you."

Startled, Trish jumped and spun around, hoping the guilt at her thoughts didn't show in her face. "I was just thinking."

"I know. Me, too. I keep thinking about Selena. When I woke up this morning, I thought maybe this was all a bad dream. I pinched myself hard, but it didn't go away."

And sitting around brooding wasn't making this any easier on Gina. "Let's go horseback riding," she said, surprising herself.

"Really? You'll go riding with me?"

"Of course, but we need one of the male wranglers to go with us."

"Let's ask Jim Bob."

Another unfamiliar name. "Who's Jim Bob?"

"One of the wranglers. He is so funny. You should see his imitation of Britney Spears."

"I can't believe I've missed that. We should definitely ask Jim Bob if we can find him. But he may be busy."

"If he is, let's ask Zach."

"I don't see why not. And put your bathing suit on under your shorts. There's a swimming hole not far from the house. Perhaps we can stop and take a swim."

"Zach mentioned that yesterday. He said they have a rope so you can swing out and drop in the middle. He says the water's cool, too, even in the summer."

"Cool sounds good."

"Will you swim, too?"

"If Lenora can find a bathing suit around here somewhere that fits me. I'll check on that while you look for Zach."

And if Zach couldn't make it, they'd find someone else to take them. She and Gina both needed a diversion. The swimming hole would bring the memories crashing down again, but then so did everything at Jack's Bluff. She'd just have to deal with it. Ten minutes later, with a bathing suit that Lenora had appropriated from Becky's closet under Trish's freshly laundered shorts, Trish was ready to ride.

Gina was waiting at the back door. "I couldn't find Jim Bob, but Zach wants to go. And guess what? Langston's coming, too."

Trish's heart plunged to her toes right along with her confidence at handling the situation. She probably could have handled the memories, but Langston in a bathing suit in a place where they'd made love for the very first time might push her over the edge. But then she wasn't likely to jump his bones in front of Gina and Zach.

"Are you coming, or not?" Gina called. She was already out the door and walking to the stables.

"She's coming," Langston called, as he strode around the side of the house. He grabbed Trish's arm as he passed and tugged her along. "Gina needs the sunshine and release," he said. "We all do."

She couldn't argue with that.

THE HORSEBACK RIDE HAD BEEN invigorating, but it was her daughter's squeal of pleasure as she let go of the rope and plummeted into the water that was balm to Trish's soul. It amazed her that Gina could go from last night's moroseness over the whole murderous affair to this morning's excitement, but she supposed it wasn't that out of line considering the usual hormonal mood swings Gina experienced.

And a few hours of laughter didn't mean she wouldn't still experience times when the grief would hit and seem almost unbearable. It had been that way for Trish when she was only seven. Only the grief had lasted years and the nightmares were still with her.

Trish stepped to the water's edge.

"What are you waiting on, Mom? Kick off those shorts."

"In a minute."

Zach had already stripped to his bathing suit and was demonstrating the fine art of rope gripping. Langston had unsnapped his shirt and it swung open as he walked toward her, revealing a sprinkling of dark hairs that made a V toward his waist. "You did a good job with her, Mom. She's a good kid. Sensitive, but full of life."

"She is pretty remarkable," Trish agreed.

"It must have been difficult raising her on your own, with no husband to help out."

"Sometimes."

"Mom." Gina stretched the word into several syllables. "Are you coming in or not?"

"You're being paged," Langston said. He shrugged out of the white Western shirt and wiggled out of his jeans, leaving nothing to cover his magnificent body but a pair of light blue swimming trunks. She watched as he walked to the water and waded in. He still had the swagger, only now it reeked of power instead of youth.

She turned away and stripped to the borrowed black tank that fit a little too snuggly across the breasts.

Trish folded her jeans neatly and lay them beside the clothes that Gina had carelessly tossed into a pile. This was no big deal, she told herself. Just a quick swim to break the tension of a situation she seemed to have lost all control over.

But when she looked up and caught Langston staring at her, warning signals went off in her head and skittered along her nerves. There was a line she couldn't cross with Langston and still keep things in perspective. And coming back to this spot with him was pushing her extremely close to that line.

She walked faster, shivering as she hit the water, then dove beneath the surface and started swimming away from Langston. She swam until her breath burned in her lungs, then waded out of the water and dropped to a grassy spot in the sun. Minutes later, Langston joined her, water glistening on his bronzed chest and dripping from his dark hair. Her heart hit a few erratic beats.

"It's been years since I've been in the family swimming hole," he said.

"You probably have a pool at your condo complex."

"I do, but I seldom use that, either. There never seems to be time. The oil business is booming these days, and that means long hours and lots of projects in the works."

"I'm sorry if I've taken you from that. You really don't have to be here today. I'm fine."

"I needed a morning off."

"But not to worry about my problems."

"A man's got to worry about something. I've been trying to figure out how the video ties into the carjacking. So far, I'm batting zero."

"I think the link is Detective Packard."

"Are you sure Rivers didn't mention a video while he was in the car with you or maybe infer that you had something he wanted?"

"Admittedly, I was scared and panicked, but I think I would have remembered something like that."

"But there had to be some reason he came into your shop and talked to Selena—not once, but on at least two occasions."

"He could have been buying a present for a girlfriend or a wife."

"Or maybe making a play for Selena."

"She wouldn't have flirted with him. She loved Enrico."

"Maybe he hid the video in your shop and then when he came back for it, it was missing."

"Why would he hide it in my shop?"

"I'm just thinking out loud here, but what if someone was after him, and he just ran in off the street? He might have come back the next few times to ask Selena if she'd found it. When she hadn't, he may have figured you had it or knew where it was."

She shook her head. "If he'd asked Selena, then why wouldn't she have just asked me about it?"

"Let's just suppose that for some reason she didn't."

"Then it could still be in the shop." She stood and started to pull her shirt over her damp suit, but stopped as she realized what her next move should be. "I have to go back and look for it, Langston. If the video was ever in the Cottage Boutique, it's likely still there, maybe folded away in one of the sweaters or under some of the lingerie in the cupboards."

"It's worth looking into, but no need for you to go. I'll fly up to Dallas and search the shop."

He was doing it again, taking over her life as if she were a subsidiary of Collingsworth Oil. "I'm going with you, Langston. It's my shop, and I'll know better where to search. Besides, I'd like to look through the sales records for the past few months. If Buck Rivers or anyone else suspicious was there as a customer, we may have that information."

"It's too risky."

"It's no riskier for me than it is for you."

"If the cops drive by and find you there, they might just arrest you on the spot."

"I'm seeing them tomorrow. If they plan to arrest me, they'll do it anyway. And I can't imagine that the killer is just hanging around the scene of the crime waiting on me. Unless it's Packard."

"And then what?" Langston asked.

She reached over and patted the pistol that bulged from the jeans' pocket in the grass next to them. "Then you'll have to shoot him."

"Is that your final answer?"

"Unless you just want to beat him up."

"You know that's not what I meant."

"I'd like to search the shop before I'm questioned by the police tomorrow. If the killer is looking for me, he won't be looking for me there. Even Packard thinks I'm hiding out somewhere for my protection. If you don't take me there, I'll go on my own. So, what time do we leave?"

He shook his head. "I don't remember you're being this hardheaded when I knew you before."

"I was. You just didn't have the occasion to see it."

"I have a meeting downtown at two," he said, "but I'll be back for you at seven. And plan to spend the night. There's no use flying back to the ranch tonight only to fly back to Dallas tomorrow for the meeting with Caruthers and Detective Packard."

Plan to spend the night. The risks had just multiplied exponentially.

CELESTE STEPPED OFF THE elevator and stormed through the double glass doors of the executive offices of Collingsworth Oil. She nodded to the receptionist but didn't stop. She'd talked to Langston earlier and knew he'd come in today though he'd cancelled their date for tonight due to some unexpected complications with Trish Cantrell's situation.

It was absurd! If this "*family friend*" needed protection, then hire her a bodyguard. People of Langston's wealth and position didn't get personally involved in this sort of lowlife, criminal complication. It was degrading, not to mention dangerous.

It was the ranch mentality. Every time he went out there, he transposed into the kind of earthy, cowboy type she abhorred. It was fine for Bart and Matt. All they cared about were those acres and acres of mud and grass and a bunch of smelly cattle, but Langston had moved beyond that. He was not only accepted but sought after by some of the most elite groups in Houston society. Obviously, he needed a reminder of that.

She took deep breaths as she hurried down the halls.

Langston would see things her way if she handled this just right. But before she reached Langston, Lenora Collingsworth stepped out of Jeremiah's office and right into Celeste's path.

"Lenora, what a surprise," Celeste crooned. "Lang didn't mention you were visiting him today. Did you two have lunch together?"

"No, and actually I'm not visiting. Jeremiah has named me as acting CEO of Collingsworth Enterprises until he's able to return to his duties."

"Jeremiah named you as his replacement?"

"You sound surprised. Didn't Langston tell you?"

No, and stunned was more the word. "You can't seriously be thinking of filling the position."

"I'm not planning any major upheavals in the enterprise's operations, but, yes, I am planning to take the position seriously. New blood and a woman's intuition can't be all bad."

"What about Langston?"

"Nothing's changed with Langston. He's still president of Collingsworth Oil. He'll just be running major decisions by me instead of Jeremiah."

"But you have your life, your charities, your family."

"This is only temporary. I'm sure the charities and my family will survive. Change is a part of life."

And things were certainly changing fast around here. If anyone was taking Jeremiah Collingsworth's position, it should be Langston. And if he weren't running around playing cowboy hero to a shopgirl, he'd be here seeing to it that he was acting CEO.

"Lang's expecting me," Celeste lied. "I should run,

but good luck with the new responsibilities." She faked a smile and forced a civility to her tone that she didn't feel.

"Actually, I don't think Langston is in his office, Celeste. He left a few minutes ago to go back to the ranch."

"Back to the ranch? Is this connected with Trish?"

"I'm sure Langston will explain everything to you."

"You know, Lenora, I'm surprised that you would take this woman into your house and encourage your sons to become mixed up in a situation that reeks of danger. You must know Trish very well to take such risks for her."

"We know her well enough."

"Then I suggest you have your other sons take some of the responsibility for protecting her and solving her problems. Langston is a very busy man with far more important responsibilities."

"If you have any issues with Langston, Celeste, you need to take those up with him."

"You're absolutely right." And she would. In fact, she'd be driving to Jack's Bluff immediately to do just that. This nonsense with Trish Cantrell had gone on long enough. She would put a stop to it now!

Chapter Nine

Gina wandered into the kitchen where Juanita was rolling dough and Jaime was perched on a stool, drinking a glass of soda and skimming the latest issue of *Glamour*.

"This girl looks kind of like you, Gina," Jaime said, pushing the magazine to the edge of the counter so that Gina could get a better look.

"I wish."

"No, she does. I'll bet if I did your makeup, we could make you look just like her."

Juanita brushed her hands on her apron and walked over to see the picture. "Humph. Too much makeup. You wear that much, people think you are *mujerzuela*."

"Oh, no! You wouldn't want that," Jaime said, faking horror.

Juanita went back to her dough. "You show *mucho*. Men lose interest. They like to guess a little, you know."

"I keep them begging," Jaime teased. "That's more fun."

Gina loved the way Jaime interacted with everyone. She might be a little on the wild side, but she was nice—and really cool.

"And this woman looks like your mother," Jaime said, pointing to the picture of a classy brunette modeling a skin-fitting white evening gown.

Gina looked at the model. "No way."

"Yeah, way. Look at her eyes and the mouth. Your mom is really pretty, but she could be hot if she wanted. I bet she used to be back when she dated Langston. He only dates good-looking women, but he's kind of dulls-ville since he started dating the witch of Houswick."

"Houswick?"

"Play on words," Jaime said. "You know, Houston instead of Eastwick. From the movie."

Gina was still clueless.

"Before your time," Jaime said. "We'll rent it one night. Anyway the witch is Celeste, Langston's new fiancée. Gorgeous and about as much fun as a bikini wax."

"Then why does he date her?"

"He's getting old and boring, I guess."

"He's not *that* old," Gina said.

"He's pushing thirty-six. I may just kill myself when I get thirty. Sorry, guess that's not funny with your friend just getting killed. You have to be bummed out about that."

"Pretty much."

"You're not scared though, are you?"

"A little," Gina admitted.

"You shouldn't be afraid," Juanita said, breaking into the conversation again. "Mr. Langston says he take care of you, he takes care of you."

"You don't have to sweat much at Jack's Bluff," Jaime agreed. "Nobody, and I do mean *nobody*, messes with my brothers. The guys at school were scared to date me when I was in high school. That's why I went out of state to college. I wanted to go somewhere no one had even heard of the Collingsworth family or Jack's Bluff."

"Jack's Bluff is an odd name for a ranch that barely has a hill, much less a bluff. Who is Jack?"

"There were a pair of Jacks, actually. My great, great—continue greats to ad nauseum—grandfather won the ranch in a card game. Ask Mother about it. She loves to tell the story."

Juanita folded over the mound of dough and gave it a pounding. "It's your heritage, Jaime. You should be proud."

The house phone rang. Jaime slid from the stool and picked up the kitchen extension. "Well, well, well," she said, when she finished the quick call. "That was Jim Bob, just calling to tell us that a guest just passed through the gate. Her highness, the witch of Houswick has arrived."

"Without Langston?" Juanita asked. "She's never done that before."

"And not here to spread cheer and good will, I suspect. All Jim Bob said was 'Jack's Bluff, we have a problem.'"

THE LAST THING TRISH HAD expected was a personal confrontation with Celeste, but now that she thought about it, she should have foreseen the possibility and been prepared for Celeste's anger. Everything she'd said had been true.

Langston was an extremely busy man and he was taking valuable time from the company to deal with her problems when she wasn't a member of the family. Actually, as Celeste had pointed out, technically she wasn't even a friend, but just someone who hadn't bothered to get in touch with him for years—not until she needed his help.

Trish took the stairs slowly as the accusations echoed through the havoc that had become her reality. It was the same reasoning she'd used with Langston, but he'd refused to listen. Now she was not only bringing danger to him and his family, but causing friction between him and his fiancée. She had to go.

But did she dare take Gina with her?

Her steps grew heavy as the answer hammered its way into her heart. Gina's safety was the first consideration, and there was nowhere safer for her than Jack's Bluff. Gina wouldn't understand Trish's going off without her, but Lenora would. She was a mother, too.

Trish went into the bedroom and picked up the pad of paper she'd been using to jot notes about the incidents of the past few days. Picking up the pen, she started a new one.

Dear Langston,
I can no longer continue to interfere in your life and that of your family. You are too much a man to ever walk away from me as long as I'm in jeopardy. But I have principles, too, and they will not allow me to endanger innocent people. I only ask that you let Gina stay here until the killer has been arrested and it is safe for us to return to Dallas. I hope you and Celeste will have a long and happy life together.
Warmly,
Trish

A stabbing pain attacked Trish's right temple as she put down the pencil. She still needed a vehicle, but there were several parked outside. She'd just have to borrow one—without permission—since asking would only lead to confrontation about her decision. Her first choice would be Bart's. Nothing like a black pickup to blend in with the other millions of trucks on Texas highways.

Now she could add thief to her resume. The DPD would love that, not that she expected the Collingsworths to report the truck as missing. They were one terrific family. Celeste was a very lucky woman.

Trish ached to give Gina one last hug, but her eyes were already brimming with hot tears, and she knew Gina would realize immediately that something was up. She grabbed her handbag—the only thing she'd left the house with the night she'd gone on the run—and crept down the back staircase, walking on tiptoe lest someone hear her sneaking out.

Bart's truck was ready and waiting, doors unlocked, keys in the ignition. She took that as a favorable omen. A quick turn and the engine hummed to life. Trish took one last look at the big house and thought of her daughter inside it surrounded by Collingsworths.

That was the only comfort she took with her as she drove the hot, dusty road to the gate.

A young wrangler with faded jeans and dark curly hair that hugged the collar of his blue Western shirt was doing gate duty, a grim reminder of the security needed to keep people safe when they opened their home to her.

He rode his horse to the passenger-side door as she lowered the window. "Howdy, Ms. Cantrell."

"Have we met?"

"No, but you're the celebrity around here. We all know who you are."

Celebrity troublemaker. She'd screwed up everyone's routine, including his. Instead of tending livestock, he was on patrol.

He tipped his white straw Stetson. "I'm Jim Bob Harvey."

She managed a smile. "I've heard my daughter speak of you."

"Yeah, she's sumpin' else that girl. Talks fifty words a minute with gusts to a hundred. But she loves those horses."

"I think she's pretty great. I'd love to talk longer, Jim Bob, but I need to go. I'm…" She hesitated on the lie. "I'm meeting Langston in Houston."

He grinned. "That sounds fun. I haven't been into the city in a month of Sundays, but you know I can't let you leave here by yourself. Bull's orders."

"Bull?"

"Bull Durham. Used to be a Texas Ranger. Now he's got all us wranglers playing cops and robbers. I'll have to get an okay from him to open the gate for you with you going out by yourself."

Fat chance he'd get that. She considered ramming the gate with Bart's truck, but figured the smiling wrangler would shoot at her. He had a pistol at his waist. But then she had a rifle right behind her on the standard Texas truck gun rack. Not that she'd dream of using it except as a persuasion tool. She reached up and wrapped her fingers around the barrel.

"I wouldn't do that if I were you, ma'am. I'd just have to take it away from you, and then you'd get all sweaty just from getting up close to me. After a day in this heat I smell like soured oats. Just ain't worth it."

"Look, I know what Bull said, but…"

Her sentence was cut off by the crack of gunfire. Jim Bob's horse whinnied and bucked, and the wrangler half fell, half jumped from the saddle. He stayed down, and when she leaned across the seat, she saw blood gushing from his shoulder.

Her heart pounded against her chest, and the blood rush and panic pushed her to action. She opened the door and used it for a shield as she struggled to pull Jim Bob into the truck.

"Get down," he ordered and shoved her head to the seat.

Pain twisted his face into hideous contortions when he tried to reach for the rifle. She grabbed it for him, pointed it out the window and fired in the direction the bullets had come.

The return fire ricocheted off the truck's hood and shattered the front windshield. She fired again and the return fire echoed around her like fireworks on the Fourth of July.

Jim Bob groaned and pushed the barrel of the gun from in front of his face. "Cavalry's arrived, Kimosabe. Save your bullets. They'll handle the Injuns."

She was too frightened to breathe, and Jim Bob was making jokes. But he was evidently right. The gunfire continued, but no more bullets hit the truck. She let the gun fall from her hand. "We have to get you to a hospital."

"For this? I've been hurt worse saddling a jumpy horse."

She didn't believe him, but the bleeding had slowed. That had to be a good sign. She leaned back and took a deep breath, feeling a weird sense of satisfaction along with the relief. She'd run from danger for as long as she could remember. This was the first time she'd ever fought back.

LANGSTON SPED THE LAST FEW miles to the ranch, his blood pressure approaching the boiling stage as his speedometer approached lethal limits. He'd just gotten off the phone with a hysterical Gina, who'd read him an idiotic note that she'd found on the dresser in the guestroom where Trish had been sleeping.

Principles. Where the hell were Trish's principles sixteen years ago when she'd made love to him like she couldn't get enough? At least this time she'd left a note. For that he should probably send flowers.

He was almost to the gate when he heard the siren. He slowed and pulled over. Another speeding ticket. He'd definitely send flowers. And then Trish could damn well walk out of his life again with his blessings since she was hell-bent on doing it anyway.

But it was an ambulance that came up behind him and then sped past and turned in at Jack's Bluff. Trish. Her name went off like an explosion in his head. Panic all but shut down his brain as he followed the ambulance.

He saw Trish first, standing near Bart's truck. Unhurt. His heart jumped to his throat. And then he saw Jim Bob being lifted to the stretcher, his boots sticking out from under the sheet. Jim Bob saw Langston and waved.

Langston waved back, but something hard settled in his chest. He wouldn't be sending flowers, at least not to Trish. But he would be setting a few things straight.

AN HOUR LATER, TRISH WENT UP to her corner of the big house and fell across the bed. She'd survived her first shootout and so had Jim Bob. Matt had just called from the hospital with the report that Jim Bob was in surgery having a bullet removed from a muscle mass in his shoulder, but that he'd be back punching cattle in no time.

She hadn't had a chance to talk privately with Langston, but she'd felt his gaze boring into hers all the while she'd explained the exchange of gunfire to him and his family. Bart was the only one who'd questioned her reason for being at the gate in his truck, and Langston had silenced him with a look.

She'd known then that someone had given him the note. When she saw the expression on Gina's face, she knew it had been her and that she was disappointed in Trish. So much for honesty being the best policy.

But at least now even Langston must know that her leaving was the only solution. As if on cue, he stepped into her bedroom and closed the door behind him. He strode across the room and tossed the now-crumpled note to the bed. "Get over it, Trish."

She pulled herself to a sitting position. "What's that supposed to mean?"

"This isn't about Celeste or your principles. It's not even about you and me, at least not about our past relationship. It's about your inability to take genuine help when it's offered—no strings attached."

"I'm not your responsibility."

"You're not playing with amateurs, Trish."

"Don't you think I know that?"

"You don't act like you do. I had Buck Rivers's background investigated. Before he moved to Dallas four years ago, he lived in New Orleans and in New York and Miami before that. He didn't have a rap sheet in those places. He had a career. The unofficial, but reliable, report is that he was an assassin for the Mafia, until he botched a hit."

Trish's head started to spin. Not again. This could not be happening again. She started to shake and leaned against the wall for support.

Langston put a hand on her shoulder, but she pulled away. This wasn't about a carjacking or a video or even a crooked policeman. It was her past. It was never going to let go. And even Langston Collingsworth couldn't change that.

"I'm leaving for Dallas, Trish. If you want to go, be at the car in ten minutes. If you're not there..." He sputtered, his anger swallowing his words. "If you're not there, I'll hog-tie you and make sure you're still at the ranch when I get back." Langston turned and stamped out of the room.

She'd never seen him so angry. Nothing would stop him—nothing but the truth. Before the night was over, she'd make sure that he heard it.

She hurried to tell Gina goodbye. She was going back to Dallas and to the scene of the brutal, murder. "I'm sorry, Selena," she whispered. "I should have known I could never escape them."

DETECTIVE GARY PACKARD LEFT the gentleman's club in downtown Houston and took the freeway to the area near the Cottage Boutique. He slowed as he passed the shop, then pulled his unmarked car in the parking lot about fifty yards away from the front door. He settled in to stay a spell the same way he had last night. Sooner or later, Trish Cantrell would show up. He stretched and got comfortable as a streak of lightning flashed across the night sky.

His cell phone rang. The ID indicated the call was from the dispatcher at the station. He took the call.

"We have a reported spotting of Trish Cantrell."

"Does it sound like another crank?"

"No. It's a police officer. He lost her in traffic, but he's pretty sure it was her, and you'll never guess who she's with."

Gary listened and smiled. This was as good as it got.

Chapter Ten

The night was warm and muggy with lightning flashing through the clouds off to the north and the distant rumble of thunder adding bass to the high whine of the crickets and tree frogs. The condensation from Lenora's iced tea dripped onto her fingers. She hadn't taken more than a couple of sips. Billy Mack had nearly finished his beer.

He was sitting on the top step of the front porch with his back against the support column. Lenora was in one of the wooden rockers a few feet away.

"Let's not talk anymore of this afternoon's shooting," she said. "My sons have already talked it to death."

"Fine by me," he agreed, adjusting his position. "But you still look worried."

"I always worry when Langston's piloting his Cessna."

"Bad night for flying, especially if he was going north."

"He was, but he should have landed before the storm."

"So his piloting the plane isn't all that's on your mind?"

"You're starting to read me too well, Billy Mack."

"We've been neighbors from hell to breakfast."

"And I still don't understand half you say." She smiled at his turn of speech in spite of her heavy heart. Billy owned the ranch just to the west of Jack's Bluff, and he and his wife Millie had been the first neighbors Lenora had met when she'd married Randolph. She and Millie had become best friends, and Millie had taught Lenora a lot about being married to a Texas rancher. Mostly they'd laughed and cried together over their kids—and shared a bottle or two of wine when the situation called for it.

Millie had died three years ago. Billy was still grieving. Lenora understood. It was like that when you lost a soulmate. But who would want to be married to someone who wasn't—which was part of the reason she felt so down tonight.

"I know opposites attract," Lenora said, thinking out loud. "But do you think they can make a marriage work?"

Billy Mack cocked his head to one side and grinned. "Is that a proposal?"

"In your dreams. I was thinking about Langston."

"What did his socialite princess do to upset you now?"

"It's not so much what she says or even what she does. It's her attitude while she's saying or doing it. I ran into her today at the office."

"At the office? You're taking this CEO position seriously, I see."

"I'm giving it a shot."

"Good for you. So what happened with Celeste?"

"There's always an undercurrent with her, as if what

she's saying doesn't match what she's thinking. It's hard to explain, but I get bad vibes about my son being joined with her till death do they part."

"Is that still in the vows? I thought maybe they'd changed it to till the first one gets an itch the other can't scratch."

"I'd hate to see a divorce in his future, especially since he's waited this long to think about marriage."

"You make him sound old. What is he now, thirty-four?"

"Thirty-five. And I want grandchildren. Lots of them. Someone needs to get to work on that, but I'm not sure I want Celeste to be the one to give them to me."

"This doesn't have anything to do with the reappearance of Langston's old girlfriend, does it?"

"Not directly."

"That's a major concession for you. You were ready to go after Trish with both barrels when she walked out on Langston."

"I was angry for a long time. I blamed his falling apart and dropping out of UT on her, but it all worked out for the best. The Air Force Academy and his time in the service did a lot toward making him the man he is today. And then there's Jaime."

"How does Jaime fit into this?"

"She's broken a steady stream of hearts, and yet one day she's going to make some man a terrific wife. Maybe not anytime soon."

"If it's grandchildren you want, Trish would fill the bill. She comes with a ready-made one."

"I like Gina, but that's not the method to my

madness. I remember how crazy Trish and Langston were about each other. They literally glowed when they were together." Lenora sipped her tea. "I don't see that when Langston and Celeste are together."

Billy shook his head. "That might be because they're not nineteen with their heads in the clouds. Don't go interfering with a man's love life, Lenora. It's never welcome."

"I'm not going to interfere."

"Right. And this week isn't going to have a Saturday. Now what about the rest of the situation that brought them back together? Anything new with that?"

"No, and I think this is hardest on Trish's daughter. Gina is such a good kid—curious, intelligent and mature for her age."

"I can see that you've got Trish and Langston all but married again and Gina fitting into the family—all that in just two days."

"I'm a fast woman."

His eyebrows arched. "Do tell."

"You know how I meant that."

"All too well. I'm going have to make fast tracks myself. I've got a long day tomorrow. Fellow over near Austin is selling off some of his Angus stock. He's letting me have first crack at them." He stood to go. "You take care, Lenora. And tell Langston if there's anything I can do for him, give me a call."

"I'll do that."

He tipped his Stetson, waved and was gone. Lenora finished her tea. Billy was probably right that she shouldn't interfere, but even if Trish and Langston weren't ready to admit it, she was convinced that there was still a bit of the magic between them. Lenora was about to go back inside when Gina joined her on the porch and plopped down in the spot Billy Mack had just vacated.

"I wish my mom and Langston weren't spending the night in Dallas."

"I'm sure they're fine," Lenora said, voicing what both she and Gina wanted to believe. "Langston wouldn't have let Trish go along if he thought he was putting her in harm's way, not after this afternoon's experience."

"Bart says Langston's not afraid of anything."

"Nothing that I know of," Lenora admitted, this time telling the truth. "He was riding bucking broncs in high school, and he once took on a wildcat that had attacked his dog. His weapon of choice then was a BB gun. I think he was eight at the time."

"Cool. How come he stopped riding broncs?"

"I suspect he liked the way he looked with teeth in his mouth."

Gina laughed. "So, he's smart, too."

"Yes, so you don't need to worry. He'll take good care of your mother."

"She's smart, too. They'll probably take care of each other."

"I like the way you think, young lady."

"Jaime and I were talking today about how the ranch got its name. She said I should ask you about it because you love telling the story."

"Jaime pokes fun because I think it's romantic, but she'll fall in love one day, and then she'll get it."

"I'm not in love, but I'd like to hear it."

Lenora rocked back and forth slowly. "My husband's

great-great-grandfather, Calvin Collingsworth, lived in England in the late 1800s. He was poor, but dashingly handsome—so says the entry in his wife's diary. He worked in the kitchen at the castle of a wealthy duke. The duke's daughter, who was engaged to a direct descendent of the throne, saw Calvin and it was love at first sight."

"Wow! How old was the duke's daughter?"

"Sixteen, but don't get any ideas. They married far too young back then. When the duke heard of the development, he ordered Calvin never to come near his castle or his daughter again."

"What did they do?"

"She sneaked out of the castle and met him. They got caught and Calvin was thrown into prison."

"Just for seeing her?"

"For being with a woman betrothed to royalty. But she helped Calvin escape and the two of them stowed away on a merchant ship bound for America. The ship encountered storm after storm, and Calvin and Isabelle were two of less than two dozen who survived the journey. They arrived in America, battered and worn from the crossing. They were also penniless."

"So how did they get a ranch like this?"

"Calvin took odd jobs to make ends meet until one night in a rough-and-tumble Mississippi River town he won a Texas ranch in a card game. He'd bluffed his way to the win with only a pair of jacks. Thus the name, Jack's Bluff."

"And the guy actually turned over the deed?"

"Yes, but it wasn't such a big deal. The ranch Calvin won was just a few acres of wooded land in the middle of nowhere. Colts Run Cross didn't exist. Houston wasn't the huge city it is now back then, either. It was what they called a cow town, a place where the ranchers and farmers went for supplies."

"Hard to believe," Gina said. "Houston's the fourth largest city in the U.S."

"And Calvin's little plot of wilderness is now the second-largest ranch in Texas. Calvin increased his land holdings considerably as did the succeeding generations of Collingsworths. But the real boost came in 1920 when they struck oil on the land."

"Just like *The Beverly Hillbillies*."

"More like lucky Texans. The Collingsworths started out Englishmen, but they are as Texan as you can get now."

Gina hugged her knees to her chest. "That's a great story, especially the part about the two lovers getting together despite all odds."

"I like to think of true love as the real Collingsworth legacy," Lenora said, letting too much melancholy sneak into her voice and getting depressed all over again. She wanted all her children to have the kind of love and marriage she and Randolph had had.

So far it hadn't worked for Becky, though Lenora wasn't giving up hope that Becky and Nick would work things out. She knew they loved each other. She wasn't giving up on Langston, either.

"What do you say we go in and have some ice cream?" Lenora suggested. "We can probably even round up the ingredients for a hot fudge sundae."

"Sounds good to me. And maybe by the time we're through snacking, we'll hear from Mom and Langston."

"Maybe, but even if we don't, I'm sure they're fine," she said again, this time offering a silent prayer that it was true.

A CAR HAD BEEN WAITING WHEN Langston touched down his small jet at Dallas Executive Airport. They'd beaten the storm, but the sky was overcast and the wind gusting. Once they had left the airport, he'd pulled onto a side road, where they'd sat in the car and eaten deli sandwiches and chocolate chip cookies from the picnic lunch that had been packed and waiting for them in the car. Langston had excellent connections.

They'd washed down the food with cold sodas and finished just as a light rain started to fall. They'd hung out there until dark. She'd tried to muster the courage to tell him about her past, but every time she tried, his cell phone had rung, and he'd become engrossed in a new conversation. Or maybe she was just copping out again.

Matt had called a couple of times to offer updates on Jim Bob's steadily improving condition. Bart had called once, and Bull and Langston had talked at least four times. The news was that they hadn't found the shooter, but they'd discovered tire prints and a cut in the fence where they assumed he had gained access to the property. Tracks indicated he'd driven the truck to within two hundreds yards of the gate and had walked the rest of the way, sticking to an old riverbed where the trees and underbrush grew thick.

Bull felt certain the man hadn't been there long and that he'd cleared out fast when the security team had started firing back. Bull had assured Langston that things were under control now. It was a safe assumption the man had been gunning for Trish. But who was the shooter? He seriously doubted it was Detective Packard.

By the time they finally drove into town and neared the boutique, the rain was falling in sheets and the sky was the backdrop for a spectacular lightning display, a typical Texas summer thunderstorm.

"The streets are practically deserted," Langston said as he made the turn that put him in front of the strip center. "The café is the only business that looks open, and there's only one car in front of it."

Trish nodded but her attention was focused on the Cottage Boutique. With the lights in the bay windows turned off, the cottage appeared stark and lonely, almost sad. The look changed to eerie when a streak of lightning illuminated the bright orange police tape stretched across the door.

The scene of the crime. Selena's murder. An icy chill slithered up Trish's spine. It felt incredibly like a warning. She ignored it. "I have the remote to the garage door that I took from my wrecked car in my handbag."

"Good. That will keep us from getting drenched. I just want to make sure there are no signs of anyone watching the shop, though I don't expect there to be."

"A comforting assumption. I'm not sure how you reached it."

"Assuming today's shooter is Selena's killer, he's not going to have rushed back here so that the police can pick him up."

"Did you report the shooting at your ranch to the DPD?"

"Not yet, but he doesn't know that. And your Gary Packard thinks you're somewhere else."

"And exactly why would he think that?"

"Because Aidan Jefferies called in a report that he'd spotted you in south Texas driving toward Mexico with Selena's boyfriend."

"Why would he say I was with Enrico?"

"He didn't say you were with Enrico. He described Enrico, which gave the report a lot more credence, especially since Enrico told them he was going to visit Selena's family in Mexico."

"I guess you heard that from Aidan as well."

"No, I got that from Caruthers. He left the info on my answering machine along with the message that he'll be in Dallas all day tomorrow and will pick you up for your interview with Detective Packard."

Langston did have a wealth of resources at his command. "Aidan's a cop. Couldn't he get in trouble for lying to the DPD?"

"Aidan, lie? He wouldn't do that. He just made a mistake. He'll call them back and report his error as soon as I call and tell him we're out of here."

"He must be a very good friend."

"One of the best. And he owed me one. I saved his life a few years back when the boat we were fishing in capsized. He hit his head on the side of the boat and was knocked out. I kept him afloat on the overturned fishing rig until we were rescued."

He circled the block again, and then pulled up in the drive as Trish pushed the button to open the garage door. Once inside, she closed it quickly but took her time getting out of the car. She dreaded what she'd find inside.

The police markings. The blood. The horrid evidence that her employee—and friend—was no longer alive.

She opened the back door to the shop with the key and stepped inside. Langston was a step behind her.

He pressed a small flashlight into her right hand. "Use this, and try to keep the beam away from the window, though with the lightning show going on, I doubt it would draw attention."

Trish flicked on the light and pointed the beam toward the floor. "Where shall we start?"

"Wherever you think best."

"Then let's start in what we call the sitting room. It's the first room you come into when you enter the shop. If Buck Rivers dashed in to hide a video, it seems likely he'd have stashed it there."

"Sounds reasonable," Langston agreed.

Which was fine except that the path from the garage to the sitting room led past the office where Selena had been shot. The door was closed and banded with police tape. Trish leaned against the wall, fighting off a wave of nausea.

Langston placed an arm around her shoulder.

"I'm okay," she whispered. She had to be—for now. Leaning on Langston for support would add more emotional stress than she could bear. Forcing her legs and her stomach to steady, she pulled away from him and led the way to the area where the latest lines of designer jeans, shirts, cropped pants and sundresses were on display.

The mannequins had a surreal quality about them when caught in the flashlight's beam, as if they might suddenly turn on their own and point to the hidden video.

"I'll go through the clothes displayed in the antique wardrobe," she said, aiming illumination in that direction.

"I'll start on the other side of the room."

She knew something was wrong the second she started handling the clothes. "Someone's moved things around. The styles aren't grouped correctly, and these sweaters aren't folded the way we do it."

"Maybe Selena made some changes the day you were at the camp."

"No. Someone's handled everything. Whoever searched my house for the video must have also broken into the shop."

"They did a much neater job of searching," Langston said. "But then they could have had a lot more time."

"Not if it was the man who killed Selena. She pushed the silent alarm, and the killer had to clear out quickly."

"Unless he'd already searched before she arrived."

"Every time we find what should be a clue, the evidence becomes more confusing. One step forward, a dozen steps back."

"When we get the right clue, it will all fit," Langston said.

"You are a lot more confident of that than I am." She went back to the task at hand, though it was hard to keep up her hopes of finding the video now. If it was here, someone had likely already recovered it. Still, she handled each piece of clothing, using her sense of touch as much as sight to search for a video between the folds of fabric.

They worked through each room, leaving no niche, cranny or shelf untouched. By the time they got to the bridal parlor, a room that had once been a study, she'd developed a nagging ache at both temples.

"It's not here, Langston," she said. "It was a terrific theory, but the video's just not here."

"Have we covered every room?"

"All but the lingerie." And she wasn't looking forward to looking through silky, suggestive unmentionables with Langston.

"Lead the way," he said. "We've covered this much. There's no use in stopping now."

Agreed. What was a couple of lacy teddies compared to the importance of locating the video? She was growing less sure by the minute that the video had ever been more than a ruse to throw the police off target. Assassins didn't need a video as an excuse to go after her. They'd been doing it for most of her life. She'd been foolish to ever believe that could stop.

"It's nearly 2:00 a.m.," Langston said, when they'd finally covered the lingerie area from top to bottom. "Are you up to looking through the business records?"

"I'd like to at least check the sales receipts and see if Buck Rivers was actually a customer, though I dread going into the office where…"

"You don't have to," Langston answered when she hesitated. "Tell me what records you want, and I'll get them for you. We can take them with us and analyze the data in the morning."

"Take them with us where?"

"We have a suite at the Hilton in my name. We're already registered. The key is in the glove compartment of the car."

"You think of everything."

"I try. So, what do you want to take with us, though

I'm pretty sure the police will have already obtained a warrant and taken what they wanted."

"Like the computer?"

"Most likely. Do you have backup disks?"

"Yes, and hard copies of the sales receipts and customer information." She told him what items to get, then waited near the door to the garage while he retrieved them. She was wimping out, but if she faced the crime scene tonight, she'd never sleep, and she needed to be alert for the police questioning tomorrow.

Langston met her at the door a few minutes later, files in hand. "Let's get out of here," he said. "I could use a soft bed."

Her heart jumped and then dropped to her stomach. And here she went again, living a nightmare and still not able to crush the memories and convince her heart that it was over forever between her and Langston.

There had best be more than one soft bed.

LANGSTON SLIPPED OUT OF HIS boots and fell to the bed with his clothes on. He was dead-tired, but the second he closed his eyes, his mind jumped into overdrive and unwanted desire coursed through his body. It was the fatigue that was making his mind play tricks on him, awakening the haunting memories and stirring the sweet pangs of arousal.

He pushed the thoughts from his mind, only to have them return again and again. He desperately needed closure on his and Trish's past relationship, but this wasn't getting it.

Finally, his eyes closed and he fell into a half sleep that allowed the memories to fully infiltrate his subconscious. He and Trish were naked in the swimming hole, their slick bodies pressed against each other. And then he carried her to the shade of the oak tree and they made love on the carpet of cool grass. Made love over and over and over.

And still he ached for more.

TRISH WAS UP BY SEVEN. She showered and dressed in a pair of jeans and a white short-sleeved sweater top, another outfit borrowed from Becky's well-stocked closet. The stack of receipts were spread out on the hotel desk when Langston finally stuck his head through the door of their adjoining rooms. He'd pulled on his jeans, but not his shirt or shoes. He yawned and raked his fingers through his dark, rumpled hair, looking sexier than any man had a right to.

"I'm ordering coffee from room service. What else do we need?"

"Croissants and fruit would be nice."

"Is that it? No bacon and eggs?"

"Not for me."

He disappeared for a few minutes, and when he rejoined her, his hair had been combed and his breath smelled of minty mouthwash. His chin, however, was still dotted with dark whiskers. Virile was the description that sprang to Trish's mind. She turned her attention back to the receipts before he realized how he affected her.

"There was no record that Buck Rivers had ever made a purchase in the boutique," she said. "But we'd only have his name if he used a credit card or willingly provided his name and e-mail address to get on our mailing list."

"Did you note anything suspicious?"

"No. Most of the sales are from our regular customers."

"What about new customers? You must have had some."

"A few." She picked up one of the receipts from the shortest stack. "Mrs. Garson came in for the first time in June. She bought several outfits for a cruise to the Bahamas." Trish picked up two more receipts. "Gayle Isben came in for a sundress for her husband's company picnic. She was referred by the mayor's wife. And Mr. Carletti came in with his daughter who is getting married in August. She bought a going-away dress and several outfits for a honeymoon in Hawaii. He is a very generous father."

"Carlos Carletti?"

"Yes, do you know him?"

"I know of him. Let me see that receipt."

The waiter arrived with the coffee and croissants. Langston signed for them, then brought the tray back to her bedroom. He poured them each a cup of coffee then lifted the cream pitcher to pour.

"Just a few drops," she said.

"I remember."

Two words, and her heart skipped crazily as if he'd whispered an endearment. She sipped the coffee but decided not to taste the croissant until her stomach stopped the unwarranted fluttering.

"You have several purchases here by Carletti—" Langston said as he sifted through more of the new customer receipts "—on succeeding days."

"He came back to pick up a few additional things."

"Was his daughter always with him?"

"No."

He went back to his bedroom and returned with a small black notebook. He scanned the entries. "Looks as if Carletti's visits were followed almost immediately by Buck Rivers's visits."

"I don't know what you're getting at."

His cell phone rang. He walked to the other room to talk. The call was obviously private. Probably Celeste. She'd no doubt be furious that Langston had come to Dallas with Trish. She shouldn't be. She had Langston for life.

LANGSTON'S BODY WENT RIGID as he listened to the private detective's findings concerning Trish. "Her identity is fake?"

"I'm positive. Her social security number is completely different from the Trish Edwards who worked for Collingsworth Oil. The one she's using now belongs to a girl who died in a car wreck in Houston in 1968, but Trish Cantrell used it to collect $100,000 worth of death insurance five years ago on a man who was reportedly her father. That was just before she moved from London to Dallas and opened the Cottage Boutique.

"The social security number she was using back when you knew her was issued to a Patrice Edwards who'd died from a botched surgery in 1964. So, who knows who the woman you're with really is?"

Langston took a deep breath and exhaled slowly, letting off steam to keep from exploding. "Thanks, Clay."

"I'll keep looking, but it's going to take a while to discover everything with all these fake social security numbers floating around."

"Let it go, but I would like you to do a full background check on Carlos Carletti. See if you can find a link between him and Buck Rivers or between him and Trish."

"You got it."

Langston pulled on a shirt and marched back into Trish's bedroom.

"Would you like more coffee?" she asked.

"No, Trish. No coffee. But I would like some straight answers. You've come into my life twice now and turned it upside down both times. This time you've brought a killer with you. Now I know you're not Trish Cantrell or even Trish Edwards. I think I at least deserve to know who you are."

She backed into the unmade bed and dropped to the edge of the mattress. "You're right, Langston. You deserve the truth, but we'll have to start from scratch.

"Everything you know about me now is a lie."

Chapter Eleven

Trish took a deep breath, sat up straighter and held her head high. She didn't know what she wanted from Langston now, but she knew it wasn't pity. She met his gaze and trembled, then forced the confession from her dry throat. "I was a Mafia princess."

Langston stared at her, a stunned expression on his face. "Are you giving this to me straight?"

"I'd never make this up. My father was the oldest son of a powerful Chicago Mafia leader."

"No wonder you never talked about your family."

"He wasn't still a part of organized crime when we were dating. We'd changed our names and started new lives a half-dozen times by then."

"What is your real name?"

"I'm Trish Cantrell for all practical and business purposes. I was christened as Carolyn Marie Lombardio. Sit down, Langston. It's a long story." A painful one that would drag her back into the darkest pits of hell.

Langston pulled a chair close to the bed, as if he'd miss something if he weren't next to her and looking her in the eye. "Guess you should start at the beginning," he said.

She nodded and bit her bottom lip so hard she tasted blood. It was the first time she'd said any of this out loud. She'd hoped she'd never have to. "My father was being groomed to take over the reins from his father when I came along, though I didn't know that at the time. I only knew we were a big family with lots of cousins and that my father never talked about what he did."

"Then things were okay for a while?"

"More than okay. I absolutely adored both my parents. Things were great until my brother came along. I think that's about the time my mother must have realized exactly what she'd married into."

"Did she leave?"

"No, but I remember lying in my bed and praying they'd stop arguing. The fights would always end with his storming out of the house and her crying. It frightened me, but I didn't know then that it was the beginning of the end."

"The end of their marriage?"

"The end of life as I knew it." The terror swelled inside her as the terrifying memories took over. "My mother was pushing my father to walk away from the mob and start life over somewhere else. She didn't understand that he couldn't just walk away. It's not how it worked back then. I'm guessing it still isn't. The people on the inside know too much."

"How old were you?" Langston asked.

"Seven. We walked away from our huge house the day after my birthday celebration with all the extended family. Mother had our bags packed when I came in from school. She said we were going on a surprise trip, but I was knew something bad was happening. She'd been crying, and my father kept screaming at us to hurry. Finally, he picked me up and carried me to the car. It's strange, I know, but I remember that day like it was yesterday."

"So your father had given in to you mother's pleas."

"Yes. He explained to me much later that when he'd told his father he wanted out, my grandfather became hysterical. He told him that leaving would be suicide, that if he ran out on the 'family' they would come after all four of us and that he'd be stripped of his rank and powerless to save us."

"But still you left?"

"We did. It was the last I ever saw of my grandparents or any of my aunts, uncles or cousins. It was as if they no longer existed."

"Was there retribution?"

"Not right away. Months went by, and then…" Trish's throat closed on the words. She was sliding back in time, standing behind her mother as she went to the door with Trish's baby brother in her arms.

"My dad moved us to a small town in Oregon," she continued, her voice shaky. "He didn't think they'd find us. Then one day my mother went to the door and a man was standing there with a machine gun. She screamed at me to run, but I was too scared. I stood there while he fired over and over until my mother and the baby were…"

Obliterated. The nightmare engulfed Trish and a cold chill settled in her chest. It was as if she were seven again, standing there watching the blood from her mother's and brother's lifeless bodies pool on the beige carpet.

Langston left the chair and moved to the bed. He took her clasped hands in his. "You're cold as ice."

"I try never to think about it, but the images never fade."

"I'm sorry, Trish, really sorry. No child should ever have to see something like that. Did the man hurt you at all?"

"No, but he looked right at me before he left. I still remember his eyes, but then I've seen them in a thousand nightmares. They were vacant, like the glassy eyes of a doll."

He squeezed her hands tighter, and some of his warmth seeped into her frigid veins. "Was anyone home with you?"

"No, and I didn't go for help. I was still standing over the bodies when Dad returned hours later, in shock, I guess. He started screaming, then crying. Finally I cried, too, and it seems now that we huddled there in the horror for hours, clinging to each other and crying. Finally, he wrapped what was left of their bodies in a sheet and put them in the backseat of our car."

He kept hold of her hands, his thumbs massaging her fingers. "What did you do with the bodies?"

"I don't actually remember the rest. I must have blocked it out. When I asked later, Dad said we had our own funeral for them at the edge of the river that ran through town and then let them float into eternity."

"Did you move from the house?"

"That very night. The next day my father called the FBI. He agreed to give them vital information on the workings of the organization in exchange for putting the two of us in protective custody. He told me later that at that point and for years later, he wanted to die. He hung on for me."

"He was a very brave man."

"He was the bravest man I ever met, right until the end."

"When was that?"

"Five years ago, when I moved to Dallas."

"Were you still in protective custody the summer we met?"

"No, we'd been released a year earlier. By then the mob as my dad knew it had pretty much disintegrated. His father was dead and there had been lots of shake-ups in the hierarchy. The stakes had been upped, but the game and the players had changed. The Justice Department declared it was safe for us to be on our own again, and we moved from a small Montana town to Houston. My dad went to work for UPS. I attended the spring semester at the University of Houston and took a summer job with Collingsworth Oil."

"I would have never guessed. You seemed so happy."

"I was happy, Langston, happier than I'd ever been in my life. I thought the danger was over. I thought I could make a life for myself, make friends without worrying that I would inadvertently give something away and put either my father or me or both of us in danger. For once in my life, I was just a normal person." She hesitated; even now, she had to tread carefully here. "You'll never know what that summer meant to me."

He loosened his hold on her hands, but his piercing gaze intensified until she felt he might literally see past her words and into her heart.

"I don't get it, Trish. If you were so happy, why did you walk away from me, your job, your college plans?"

"Because the danger wasn't over, Langston."

Langston moved from this chair to sit beside her on the bed. He put an arm around her shoulder and pulled her close, and this time she couldn't make herself fight her need to have him close.

"It will be over soon, Trish, I promise you that. But I still don't get it. Did something happen then to make you run?"

"My father got out of the car at our Houston apartment complex one night, and a man he remembered from Chicago walked up and put a pistol to his head. Dad made a surprise move and managed to knock the man off balance just as he pulled the trigger. The bullet missed him. He was alive by luck. We moved again, that time to London."

"You could have written."

"What was the point? You had it all going for you, Langston. A terrific family. Wealth. A promising career with Collingsworth Oil. I had nothing to offer but danger."

"I could have helped."

"We were nineteen. You could have gotten yourself killed, and I couldn't have lived with that on my conscience."

"You could have explained your reason for leaving."

"And if I had, would you have let me walk away? Would you have been any more reasonable then than you are now?"

"Probably not." Langston pulled away, then stood and walked to the window.

She ached to tell him how much losing him had hurt, how many nights she'd cried herself to sleep, how much she'd loved him. But she couldn't bring herself to do it then. And she didn't dare do it now.

"What made you come back from London?"

"My father had terminal cancer, and he wanted to die in America. I think he somehow thought it would make him closer to my mother. He never got over her death. I contacted the Justice Department and they said that the man who'd shot my father in Houston was just a loose cannon acting on his own and that he'd been shot and killed in a police drug sting less than a year after shooting Dad. They were certain the danger was over, and for some unknown and obviously erroneous reason, I believed them. I took the money from his only insurance policy and invested it in the boutique and a house that I hoped to make into a real home for Gina."

"You did the right thing."

"No, Langston. I did the wrong thing. I caused the death of my best friend, a smart, sweet girl who only wanted to get married to the man she loved. And now I've dragged you and your family into danger. Don't you see? It never pays to get involved with me."

"You didn't cause Selena's death. There's no proof that any of this is connected to your past. You were carjacked. The abductor had a video in his possession and some murderous lunatic assumes that since you were with him when he died, you must have the video. That could be all this is."

"Buck Rivers was a hit man for years. It makes sense that someone paid him to kill me."

She stood and walked over to where Langston was standing. This time when she met his smoky gaze, she didn't tell herself any lies. Her heart had been to hell and back over the past few minutes. The least she could do was admit the truth to herself.

She'd been in love with Langston Collingsworth sixteen years ago when she'd walked out of his life to keep from bringing danger into it. And she'd loved him every day of her life since then. It didn't change a thing. She'd have to walk away one more time when this was over. She'd go back to London or maybe Australia, somewhere she could keep Gina with her and be safe.

She'd miss him every day of her life.

"What about Gina?" Langston asked.

Her heart plunged. "What about her?"

"Does she know about the Mafia connection?"

"No. I didn't want her to grow up the way I did, afraid of every knock at the door, of every stranger she passes on the street. And there seemed no real reason to tell her. The Justice Department said we were as safe as any other American citizen. I'd forgotten how unsafe that was."

"This is coming to a head soon, Trish. Right now we just need to stay focused. I still think the video is the key. If there were no missing video, what was the point of someone breaking and entering to search your house and your shop?"

He pushed an errant curl from her cheek and let his fingers linger on her flesh. Her pulse raced, but she couldn't read anything into this except that he felt empathy for all she'd been through.

"You're lucky to be a Collingsworth, Langston. You have solid roots, a family that will always be there for you, a home you can always go back to and know you belong."

"Yeah. But a man needs more." He pulled away

quickly as if touching her were suddenly distasteful. "I should go shower."

A man needs more. His unexplained words played in her mind as he left. Was he talking about Celeste, reminding Trish that even though he'd stand by her, he was in love with someone else?

A man needs more. A woman needs more, too, Langston Collingsworth. It's just that some of us will never have it.

LANGSTON STOOD IN HIS HOTEL room with Phil Caruthers while Trish was in her room readying herself for the trip to the police station. The three of them had spent the past two hours in a conference that Langston had insisted on. The fact that Trish had ties with organized crime—even severed ones—had come as a shock. He figured that was just the kind of surprise Caruthers didn't like to get once he was into a case.

Not that this should become a full-blown case. Trish was the victim, but he could see how her story would look suspect to the police. A supposedly random carjacking but perpetrated by a known criminal who'd made several trips to her shop and had been filmed talking and laughing with Trish's employee. And then both the perpetrator and the employee wind up dead.

And if Packard suspected for even a second that she thought he could be the man who threatened her and broke into her apartment, he'd take a hard line against her. Not that it wasn't possible that Trish was right about the detective. Crooked cops were as common as the cold these days.

"I'd feel better if I were present for the police interview," Langston said.

"You have no legal right to be there," Caruthers reminded him. "You're not even on record as being a friend, and I suggest you leave it that way, especially now that we know Selena's murder could be a hit gone bad."

"I'm still hoping this is about the disappearance of a mysterious videotape and not a Mafia hit. She and Gina deserve a chance to have some normalcy in their lives."

"I agree. Have either you or Trish searched her car since the carjacking?"

"No, but I'm sure the police have searched it. If there was a video, surely they would have found it."

"Sometimes an owner does a better job of that than the police," Caruthers said, "especially when the police may not be convinced there ever was a video. I'll check with Trish. If she's interested, we can get permission to go to the impound lot and take a look."

"Do you think Gary Packard will approve that?"

"When I put it to him just right, but he may insist on going with us."

"Which means I couldn't tag along."

"That's what it means. You know, I've never gotten this relationship you have with Trish exactly straight in my mind. You say you knew her briefly sixteen years ago and hadn't seen her again until you tracked her to a deserted fishing camp three days ago."

"That's right."

"After she sent the daughter that none of you had ever met before to your house?"

"I know it sounds unusual, but I understand that a

little better now," Langston admitted. "Her past has given her reason to fear the worst and she doesn't have family or lifelong friends that she could have called on for help with Gina."

"Could be that's why she settled here in Texas, but odd that she hadn't tried to get in touch with any of you before now."

"Not so odd." Langston hesitated, but saw no reason not to level with Caruthers. "We didn't part on the best of terms."

Caruthers smiled. "Now we're getting to the nitty-gritty. You were lovers, right?"

"No wonder you're a good defender. Nothing gets by you."

"Not much. I'd say you were probably really into her sixteen years ago."

That was the understatement of the century, but close enough. And made this a good time to change the subject. "I'd like to fly back to Houston tonight. Any reason why Trish won't be able to do that?"

"No, I'm sure Packard won't arrest her since she's cooperating. If he did, I'd have her out in a matter of hours anyway, and he knows it. I will insist on getting a copy of the film from the Cottage Boutique. Trish has the right of ownership to that as well."

"I'd like to take a look at it when you get it," Langston said.

"I'll give you a call."

"I'm ready," Trish said, joining them.

"Then I guess there's nothing left to say, but good luck," Langston said.

"She won't need luck with the interrogation," Caruth-

ers said. "That's what you're paying me the big bucks
for."

Still Langston felt anxious the second Trish stepped out
of his sight. He picked up his phone and called Melvin.
Work could always be counted on to claim his mind.

"I hope you're getting back to Houston soon,"
Melvin said. "There were two men from the CIA in the
office a few minutes ago."

"What did they want?"

"They said they can only discuss their concerns with
you. They'll be back tomorrow."

Langston groaned. Could his day possibly get any
more screwed up? His phone beeped. Someone was
trying to call in. His apprehension level soared. It could
be Trish. Something could have gone wrong.

"I have another call. I'll get back to you." He switched
over. "Hello."

"Where are you, Langston?"

Celeste, with irritation dripping from her voice. Well,
there you go. His day could and probably would
become significantly more screwed up. And it was still
hours before dark.

LANGSTON HAD FOUND IT impossible to sit at the hotel
and do nothing while he waited for Trish and Caruthers to return, so he decided a drink at the gentleman's
club where Buck Rivers had worked as a bouncer was
in order. He hadn't been to that type of club in several
years. If he was going to hang out in smoky joints, he
preferred one of the bars in Colts Run Cross, a bar like
Cutter's where girls danced on the floor or maybe even
on the bar—but never in your lap.

He hadn't even been to Cutter's lately. Between work and the endless social engagements Celeste dragged him to, there was seldom time to even spend an evening with his brothers.

It was a short drive from the hotel to the club. In less than ten minutes he'd pulled into the valet lane and was getting out of his car. The temperature outside was in the high nineties, but the air conditioning in the club was running full-blast. So was the sound system. He didn't recognize the song.

A hostess in what looked like black panties and a red sequined scrap of fabric across her more than ample breasts met him at the door. "Welcome," she said. "What can we do for your pleasure today?"

"I'll just have a drink in the main bar."

"Would you like a table?"

"I would, preferably not too close to the speakers."

"But close to the action." She winked as if they'd shared a special secret, then led him to a table about midway to the back. He took the seat and scanned the area. There were two girls on the curved stage, grinding away to the beat of the strident music. The bar seats closest to the dancers were about half-full. Not bad for a Thursday afternoon.

There were several groups of guys at the tables—fortunately no one he recognized. He wasn't sure exactly what he hoped to gain from this venture, but his mind was far too occupied with Trish's problems to make idle conversation.

His waitress came over, made some seductive moves and took his order for a tall ginger ale. He never drank alcohol when he was piloting the plane. As soon as she walked away, one of the dancers left the stage and slithered and swayed her way back to his table. He took a few twenties from his wallet and fanned them across the table.

"You're new in here," she said.

"You're observant."

"Can't miss a guy as sexy as you are."

"I'm flattered."

She leaned over to give him a closeup view of the almost-exposed nipples. "Are you looking for anything special?"

He slid one of the twenties into the string of fabric that served as her waistband. "Actually, I have a couple of questions about someone who used to work here."

"Who would that be?"

"Buck Rivers."

She straightened and stepped away. "Are you a cop?"

"Me? No way. What made you think that?"

"You look like a cop."

"You get that many cops in here that you know them by look?"

"We get our share."

"I'll bet. One of my friends is a cop, a detective. Name's Gary Packard. Great guy. Do you know him?"

She propped both hands on her shapely hips. "No, I don't know anyone. I'm just here to dance." That said, she moved on to the next table without giving him or his twenties a backward glance.

Langston finished his drink and was about to leave when someone he did recognize walked in and took a table in the far back corner of the room where there was no one else around. Carlos Carletti, Trish's big spender. Langston had not only heard of him as he'd told Trish, but he'd seen his picture in the paper several times last year when the man had been involved in a gambling scandal in New Orleans. Which meant he might possibly have ties to organized crime.

Under the circumstances, Langston hadn't wanted to mention the fact to Trish, but now it was at least possible that he also had ties to Buck Rivers—or at least access to him.

Langston finished his ginger ale and took his leave, but his mind was working overtime now, trying to sort out and slot the new information that might or might not be pertinent to Trish's situation.

THE POLICE INTERVIEW HAD TAKEN just under two hours, but walking away from the station with Caruthers, Trish couldn't see that her situation had changed in any significant way.

"The detective is obviously still under the illusion that I was something more to Buck Rivers than a victim," she said as Caruthers opened the car door for her.

"It sounded that way or at least he was trying to decide if it was possible. What's your take on him now?"

"I'm not sure what you mean."

"Do you still think he was the one who broke into your apartment?"

She sighed. "I'm less sure of that. I saw the intruder only for a few seconds, and he was wearing a mask."

"But at the time you believed it was Packard."

"I was certain of it."

"You're not letting the fact that Buck Rivers was a hit man at one time influence your feelings on that are you?"

"Maybe. It's just that none of this makes sense. We

don't even know if the video, the carjacking and Selena's murder are connected. Maybe it's just one big bizarre coincidence."

Caruthers gunned the engine and pulled into traffic. "One thing you can count on in this business is that if something seems too coincidental to be true, it probably is."

Trish sighed and buckled her seatbelt as Caruthers pulled into traffic. "How do you think our searching my car is going to help?"

"I'll let you know after we see it."

"You did score there," Trish admitted. "Packard obviously didn't think our going to the impound site was a good idea. And you got a promise from him to have a copy of the film from my shop delivered to your office."

"Then I guess I earned the four thousand dollars Langston paid me for accompanying you."

"Whoa. You make two thousand dollars an hour?"

"I'm good, not cheap."

"If you're that good, get us another detective to work with," she suggested.

"No way. The best way to know what Packard is up to is to keep him on the case and visible."

"Then you think it's possible he's the one who broke into my house?"

"He's a cop. They come in all flavors, just like the general population. Good, bad, indifferent—and sometimes downright nasty."

TRISH DIDN'T RECOGNIZE HER CAR at first. When she did, the sight made her physically ill. What used to be her almost new, white Toyota was a muddied, squashed piece of metal. The damage looked ten times worse here in this concrete cemetery of cars than it had in the ditch.

"You were lucky to walk away from that," Caruthers said.

"I didn't realize it was wrecked that badly."

"That's because we drove off before the tow truck driver pulled it from the ditch," Packard said, joining them, though she hadn't noticed him approaching.

She walked to the mangled door and looked inside. There were bloodstains on the upholstery near where Buck Rivers had been sitting. Evidently his head had slammed into the window, which explained why he'd been knocked out that first few minutes.

"How long did the car sit before it was towed?" Caruthers asked.

Packard leaned against the left fender. "Does it matter?"

"I'd just like to know if someone other than you and the officer who responded to Trish's 9-1-1 call had access to the car."

"No. I thoroughly checked the area before I left. Believe me, if there had been a videotape there I would have seen it. And the trooper who answered Trish's 9-1-1 call stayed with the car until it was towed. Feel free to check with him."

Trish couldn't have been less interested in towing details. It was her car that concerned her. "Did you have to rip out the seats?"

"Routine search procedures."

"Really?" Caruthers said. "It looks a little extreme to me."

"Trish claimed someone was threatening her over a video and she thought it was tied to the abduction. We didn't want to leave any stones unturned."

Caruthers only nodded. Trish inched closer, careful to avoid jutting shreds of mangled steel. It would be useless to conduct another search at this point. Everything removable had already been removed.

Caruthers circled the car. "Did anything belonging to Buck Rivers turn up in the vehicle?"

"Not a thing."

"And I suppose you searched the area surrounding the spot where you chased and shot Rivers?"

"We were over it like white gravy on chicken-fried steak. No sign of a video."

"Guess Selena's killer must have known that," Caruthers said. "Only reason I can see why he'd break into Trish's house and then her shop was if he was looking for that video."

Packard raised his arm and checked his watch. "Are you two going to be much longer? I have a killer to catch."

"No, this does it for me. How about you, Trish? Are you satisfied that the police conducted a thorough search of your car?"

"And finished totaling it in the process."

Not that it mattered in the larger scheme of things. Losing a car was nothing compared to knowing her past had cost Selena her life. The facts might not all be in, but learning that Buck Rivers had been a mob assassin told her all she needed to know.

"Yes," she said. "I've seen enough. I'm ready to go."

Back to Langston. Back to Jack's Bluff. Then back to life on the run.

THE WEATHER HAD CLEARED AND the flight back to Houston was routine, except that the facts Trish had shared that morning seemed to have erected a new barrier between them. Caruthers had stayed long enough to explain the police interview, and Trish had lamented the damage to her car on the way to the airport.

Then she'd grown silent, a silence that had lasted the entire flight and now most of the drive back to Colts Run Cross.

Langston hadn't initiated a conversation, either, except for the nonstop dialogue that had been going on in his head. He understood now that he and Trish had lived lives as opposite as two people could. He'd spent all his life on the ranch surrounded by family. She'd moved constantly as a child, afraid to make friends, afraid to even go to the door.

Langston had grown up feeling safe and knowing he belonged. Trish had grown up dealing with real-life images more terrifying than his worst nightmares.

They were totally different, but when they'd come together that summer, nothing in his life had ever felt so right. He'd been infatuated with her from the second he'd met her and totally in love with her by the end of the day. And she had loved him.

In the end, none of that had mattered. She'd run the way she had all her life. It was her heritage, the way Jack's Bluff was his. They could never have made a life together. That had to be the closure he'd been looking for.

So, why wasn't he ready to let go?

Chapter Twelve

Langston drove into Houston the next morning before breakfast and without seeing Trish. He'd lain awake for hours last night, but for the first time since Trish had arrived, it had been his current relationship with Celeste and not the old one with Trish that troubled his mind.

They were reasonably compatible, enjoyed some of the same people, and the sex wasn't bad. He'd known it wasn't love, but he'd given up on ever finding love again, had decided that he'd passed the point in life where he could lose himself that completely in someone else. So when she'd pressed the marriage issue two weeks ago, he'd agreed and taken her to pick out a ring.

But he'd never felt the kind of need for Celeste that he felt for Trish even after all these years. Marriage to Celeste was settling at best, and that wasn't fair to either of them, especially to her.

Langston took the elevator to the eighteenth floor and went straight to his office. Lynnette hadn't arrived yet, but she would have left prioritized notes concerning anything from yesterday that needed his immediate attention.

He took off his suit jacket, draped it across the hanger

and put it away. His notes were waiting. The one concerning the visit from the CIA was on top. He scanned the scanty information, basically the same thing he'd heard from Melvin. They could talk only to Langston.

He moved the note to the side. The next matter concerned his mother. She wanted a meeting with Langston to discuss changes to the company's health insurance policy. When Jeremiah recovered, Langston was going to personally wring his grandfather's neck.

He made a notation to get with the human resources director later today. He'd instruct her to meet with his mother, give her the utmost respect—and then ignore her suggestions. Hopefully, his mother would tire quickly of the pseudo-executive life. His mother was wonderful—just not as a CEO.

The next item of business was a list of phone calls to return. He was on the fifth one when Lynnette sent him an urgent buzz. He punched the intercom button.

"Celeste is here to see you."

He took a deep breath and exhaled slowly. "Send her in."

He stood when she entered. "You look great," he said, telling the truth. Celeste had the figure of a model and a superb fashion sense. She always looked as if she'd spent hours getting dressed. Frequently, she had. "Is the dress new?"

"You asked that when I wore it to lunch a couple of weeks ago."

"Guess it's not too new then."

"It really doesn't matter. I didn't stop by to discuss clothes."

She was irritated and probably here to give him a

hard time about Trish. He was tempted to just plunge in and get this over with, but it wasn't the time or the place. He offered her a seat. She refused, so he walked to the front of his desk.

"I have issues with your family, Langston."

"What kind of issues?"

"They control your life. You're constantly running out there for this one's birthday or that one's fishing trip. And once you get there you adopt their cowboy mentality. Like this thing with Trish."

"Is this about my family or Trish?"

"It's about your refusal to become independent of Jack's Bluff. You're off playing cowboy hero when you should be seizing control of Collingsworth Enterprises from your dying grandfather. You can't reach the top unless you put the ranch behind you."

He folded his arms in front of him and studied Celeste. Odd that he'd never seen this side of her before. He obviously didn't know her as well as he'd thought, but he knew who he was.

"In the first place, my grandfather is not dying, and in the second place I'm president of Collingsworth Oil because of who I am. I'm not talking about being a Collingsworth, but about my values, principles and ambition, all of which I learned growing up with my family at Jack's Bluff."

"Then you have no intention of changing?"

"I couldn't if I wanted to."

"In that case, Langston Collingsworth, I have no choice but to call off the engagement."

"If that's what you want."

"That's all you have to say?"

"What else would you have me say?"

"That you'll regret this. I was the best thing that ever happened to you."

"I could very well regret it." But he didn't think so.

"I can't believe I came this close to marrying a a... a..."

"A cowboy?"

She turned up her nose and stormed out of his office with the diamond engagement ring he'd given her still on her finger. He guessed there was no cowboy taint on it.

He was sorry it had ended this way. It didn't say much for him that he'd planned to marry a woman he'd known so little about.

Funny thing was that the thing she liked least about him and wanted him to change was the thing he liked most about himself and worried that he was losing it in the corporate world. Maybe he should go back to wearing his cowboy boots to work with his Armani suits occasionally. That would be a good reminder of where he came from.

The intercom buzzed again. "The CEO is here to see you."

He smiled in spite of himself. "Tell Mrs. Collingsworth I'm exceedingly busy but she can have ten minutes of my time."

The muffled laughter of both women was his response.

"I SAW CELESTE RUSHING DOWN THE hall," Lenora said. "She didn't even speak. Have I done something to upset her?"

"You let your babies grow up to be cowboys."

"What are you talking about?"

"Celeste broke off our engagement."

Relief surged through Lenora but quickly turned to apprehension. "Are you okay with this?"

He nodded. "It was inevitable."

And the answer to Lenora's prayers. A quick answer at that. "What was her reason?"

"Apparently I lack the proper sophistication and professional drive for her tastes."

"You? Lack sophistication? Then she must think the rest of the Collingsworths are a bunch of hicks."

"Let's just say I don't think she'll be showing up for any family reunions. Now, what did you want to see me about?"

Langston seemed fine. She wondered if that had anything to do with Trish. It would be something if they wound up together after all these years, but the shooting at the ranch worried Lenora.

"I wanted to see you about a couple of things. The most pressing has to do with the security situation at the ranch."

"What about it?"

"I'm not sure it's enough. Both Trish and Jim Bob could have easily been killed yesterday."

"I realize that. I've already talked to Bull. He's increasing the number of men on patrol. And from now on, he's assigning someone to serve as a bodyguard for you and Jaime anytime you leave the ranch. I know it's inconvenient, but it's just until Selena's killer is behind bars."

"What about bodyguards for you and your brothers? Male dignitaries and entertainers use them all the time. The President of the United States has a whole team of them."

"Okay, Mom. You're the acting CEO. You tell Matt and Bart they need a bodyguard. See if they take you seriously."

She already knew suggesting it would be a waste of breath, but that didn't mean it was a bad idea. "Trish said at breakfast that the police are no closer to naming a suspect."

"Not that they've admitted, anyway."

"I hope they make an arrest soon. I love having Trish and Gina around, but I don't like knowing it's because they're in danger."

"Don't get too attached to them. When this is over, you probably won't see them again."

Then again she just might.

"What's the next order of business?" Langston asked.

"Health insurance. I think I've come up with a feasible plan to provide it for every employee who works for Collingsworth Enterprises in any capacity and at any site."

"This is your second day in the office."

"Next week I tackle family leave policies."

Langston cradled his head in his hands and groaned. Jeremiah had created a monster.

IT WAS HALF-PAST TWO IN THE afternoon when Langston got the call from Phil Caruthers that a copy of the film confiscated by the police from Trish's surveillance camera had arrived in his office. He requested that both Langston and Trish meet him there at four-thirty.

Langston agreed to the time, though it would be pushing it for Trish. She'd need to leave the ranch within the next half hour and still might have trouble making it on time. But he was eager to get a look at the film, and he knew Trish would be, too.

One phone call to Jack's Bluff, and it was all arranged. Zach would drive Trish to Caruthers's office. Langston would drive her home. He had trouble keeping his mind on the oil business and was about to leave his office a half hour before necessary when the two gentlemen from the CIA showed up again.

"I have to leave for a very important meeting in thirty minutes," he told them once Lynnette had shown them in. "If you can say what you have to say in that time, we're in business. If not, I strongly recommend you make an appointment with my secretary."

"Thirty minutes should do for the initial contact." The younger man pulled out his wallet and flashed an ID too fast for Langston to get a good look at it.

"Can I see that again?"

"Sure." This time he left it out long enough for Langston to check his name and credentials. He checked the other agent's as well. Everything looked official, which meant nothing. Before he gave them any vital information about Collingsworth Oil he'd have Lynnette check with CIA headquarters and make sure they were authorized agents. With luck he wouldn't have to bother with that today.

"Now, how can I help you?"

"We know there's been some under-the-table money paid to a known terrorist organization in the Middle East. Indications are that it may have come from Collingsworth Oil."

"I'm not sure what you mean by 'indications' but I

can assure you that Collingsworth Oil is not in the terrorist business."

"The government would like to audit your financial records to ascertain that to be true."

"By 'the government,' are you referring to the CIA?"

"Correct. We can go through official channels and order you to allow the audit, but we prefer to avoid that. I'm sure you would, too."

"If the CIA or any other body of the United States government thinks we are investing in activities that are subversive or detrimental to the citizens of America, I'd expect them to order such an audit—once they'd shown me what they were basing their assumptions on, of course."

"Okay," the younger agent agreed, the look on his face indicating he was about to make a monumental concession. "I'll level with you."

"I'd hope so. If not you're wasting my time and yours."

"We have a reliable tip that Collingsworth Oil has been providing money and supplies to a terrorist training organization in Iraq."

Langston clenched his fists. "Who's the source of this tip?"

"I'm not at liberty to say."

"Tell you what," Langston said. "I'm a very busy man. When you're at liberty to name your source or when you have official documentation that requires our allowing you to audit this company, then you come back and we'll talk. Until then, there will be no audit."

The older agent shrugged. "I think you're making a mistake, but it's your call."

"I make mistakes from time to time. This isn't one

of them. This is the way legitimate business is conducted in America. But if I were you, I'd check that *reliable* source and see why he's giving you false information." Langston glanced at his watch. "Now, I really do have to go."

He stood, and both men followed suit. He shook their hands. "Nothing personal in my refusal," Langston said. "I know you guys are fighting a major battle with this, and I'm supportive all the way. I'm a graduate of the Air Force Academy and spent four years on active duty. As long as I'm running things, not one cent of Collingsworth Oil money will ever pass into terrorist hands."

The older agent finally managed a smile and a firm handshake. "Good to know, Mr. Collingsworth. I hope that's true and that I won't be visiting you about this issue again."

Five minutes later, Langston was in his black Porsche and fighting downtown traffic to Caruthers's office. He had high hopes for the film. It was past time Trish got a break.

TRISH LEANED IN CLOSE TO GET A better look at the slightly fuzzy image. "That's definitely the man who abducted me at gunpoint."

"Here's a better shot of him," Caruthers said. "With Selena, and they look comfortable together."

Trish checked it out. This time he was leaning over the glassed counter where she displayed the better costume jewelry. Selena was on the other side of the counter. "She's smiling," Trish said, "but that doesn't mean she knew him. She was friendly to everyone."

Langston used his laser to point out another frame.

"In this one, he's looking right at the camera, almost like he's taunting us."

"Crooks do that when they're casing a business for a robbery," Caruthers said. "They're locating the cameras so they can avoid them during the actual crime."

"Only he didn't rob Cottage Boutique," Langston noted. "He abducted Trish."

"It has to have something to do with the video," Trish said. "Maybe he was supposed to meet someone there to give them a video, or he was blackmailing them with it and using my shop for the payoff."

"You may have something there," Caruthers said. "I'm just not sure why someone thinks the video ended up in your hands or more importantly who thinks that and came after the video once Rivers was dead."

"And here's Carlos Carletti," Langston said, pointing to a new image. "When you two were at the police station yesterday, I made a visit to the club where Buck Rivers used to work. Carlos Carletti came in while I was there."

"You never mentioned that," Trish said.

"I got sidetracked before I had the chance."

She knew better. He just hadn't wanted to hit her with anything else last night.

Caruthers turned to Trish. "How well do you know Carlos Carletti?"

"Just as a customer. He came in with his daughter a couple of times last month to pay for some clothing she'd picked out for her honeymoon."

"Was that the first time he'd been in?"

Caruthers's tone made her nervous. "Yes. His daughter is a new customer. Why? What's wrong with knowing him?"

"He's bad news," Caruthers said.

Her stomach knotted. "How bad?"

"He's mixed up with some shady investors and was involved in a gambling scandal of some kind last year. I never heard how that came out, but he's obviously not doing jail time. It's rumored he has connections with organized crime."

"That's the connection we've been looking for," Trish said. "If Carlos Carletti hangs out in the club where Rivers worked, then it all but proves he paid Rivers to shoot me."

"It doesn't prove it," Caruthers said, "but it gives the theory more teeth. But Carlos may do more than hang out there. He has part interest in several clubs around the city. That may be one of them. But you have to remember that your house was broken into, Selena was murdered and you were shot at—all after Buck Rivers was dead."

"He's hired a new hit man," she said. "That's what they do. If one doesn't work out, they just get someone else."

"You're jumping to conclusions," Langston said. "Your dad broke league with organized crime when you were seven years old. What's the chance that some guy walks into your boutique after all that time, recognizes you, then goes out and hires a hit man to take you out?"

Caruthers's words came back to haunt her. *If it seems too coincidental to be true, then it probably is.* Carlos Carletti, a man with possible ties to the mafia, and Buck Rivers, a man who'd done hits for the mob before, had walked into her life at practically the same time— exactly when all hell had broken loose in her life. The events had to be connected.

Only where did the video fit in?

Langston went back to his laser, moving the red dot

to specific images. "Check out this guy. He was in the camera image with Buck Rivers on two different days and returned after Buck was killed."

"He could be the replacement hit man," Trish said. "I just wish I'd gotten a look at the shooter at Jack's Bluff."

"I wish someone had shot him," Langston said.

Trish tried to fit the new pieces into the puzzle and come up with a cohesive whole. She could almost do it, but the missing piece ruined the whole picture. The assassin theory didn't account for the mysterious video. Without that link, there was no reason for anyone to have searched her house and shop.

"I've got to drive back to Waco tonight," Caruthers said. "I'll leave these with you, but I'd suggest you two just hang loose a few days and see what hits the fan once Packard has time to study the film. In the meantime you can reach me on the cell if something comes up. And stay safe."

They left Caruthers's office and started to Langston's car for the drive back to Jack's Bluff.

"What do you say we have dinner in town?" Langston said. "I know a place where we can get a nice bottle of wine and a thick steak cooked to perfection."

"If this is a celebration of some sort I'm not in the mood."

"It's not a celebration. It's a rite of passage. I've just flunked my first authentic engagement. Celeste called it quits today."

Trish's spirits took yet another nosedive. "This is my fault, Langston. I promised Celeste I'd get out of your life and I didn't. Let me talk to her and see if I can explain."

He put a hand to the small of her back. "Forget it. It's no one's fault. We weren't in love."

His cell phone rang. He took the call. More bad news. It was written in every line of his face.

Chapter Thirteen

Gary Packard grabbed a handful of the cheap paper napkins and dabbed at the mayonnaise dripping from his bottom lip. He'd been starved when he walked in to the downtown diner but lost his appetite halfway thought the chiliburger. His town. His case. Now he had some out-of-town attorney with an ego the size of Texas pushing his nose into everything. Nothing was going to get by Caruthers.

If that wasn't bad enough, every television station in the city had made the murder of Selena Hernandez their top news story for the past two nights. Young, pretty Hispanic salesgirl murdered in an exclusive boutique in one of the most crime-free parts of the city made fascinating copy. He'd be lucky if one of the networks' news shows didn't pick it up and run with it.

That's why he had to arrest someone and fast. What he really needed was that video. He was still ninety-nine percent sure Trish Cantrell had it. She was lying about that and lying about her relationship to Buck Rivers. The scumbag hadn't been hanging out in the boutique to buy gifts for his mommy.

Buck Rivers, Selena Hernandez, Trish Cantrell and now Sam Little—the new bartender at the gentleman's club. Packard had never actually talked to Sam but he'd noticed him around over the past four of five weeks. He hadn't seemed the type to buddy up with a mean snake like Buck Rivers. But that was before Gary had spent half of today checking him out. The guy was definite suspect material.

Gary needed the video, but it might never show up. The next best thing was an arrest. He took another couple of bites of the burger, then finished his root beer and put down some change for the waitress.

Sam should be on duty by now. It was time to pay him a visit.

Thirty minutes later he was leaning against the bar, watching Sam squirt vodka into a martini glass. "It's busy in here."

Sam set the finished drink on a tray for the waitress and started on the next drink. "Place is always hopping on Thursday nights."

Sam wasn't the big bruiser Buck had been. He was leaner and had more style. Looked liked a nice enough guy on the surface, but you could never be sure about that.

"You got a break coming up anytime soon?" Gary asked.

"Why?"

"I need to talk to you."

"I'm listening."

Gary took out his wallet and flashed his credentials. "Take my word for it, Sammy. You'd rather we do our talking in private."

"What are we going to talk about?"

"A video—and those visits you made to Cottage Boutique with and without your deceased bouncer buddy."

Perspiration popped out on Sam's brow. "You got the wrong man. I've never been near the Cottage Boutique."

His next squirt went all over the place. He got nervous when he lied. That was always nice to know. "I've got a surveillance picture that says you're lying."

Sam stopped mixing drinks. "We can use one of the rooms down the hall."

"In that case, Mr. Little, lead the way." He followed Sam, but not before he picked up one of the glasses Sam had been handling, dumped the contents and slid the glass into the plastic bag in the pocket of his sports jacket.

Ten minutes later Gary Packard was certain of three things. Sam Little didn't have the video. Sam Little had no alibi for where he'd been at the time Selena Hernandez had been murdered. Sam Little was only a couple of fingerprint checks away from an arrest.

THE RESTAURANT LANGSTON CHOSE was one of his favorites. It wasn't fancy, but the walls were a mixture of exposed brick and cedar beams that gave the place a homely, old-world charm. And the acoustics were excellent, so customers could actually carry on conversations without yelling above the din.

Trish had let Langston order for them since he was familiar with the menu. He'd ordered a large rib eye, mixed-greens salad and a sweet potato soufflé—the house specialty—all large enough for sharing.

The waiter came to the table and poured a tasting sample of the imported cabernet Langston had ordered.

Langston swirled the red liquid and inhaled its fruity odor before putting the crystal rim to his lips. "Excellent."

He tried to keep his gaze and thoughts off Trish as the waiter filled both their glasses and walked away. It was a losing battle.

She looked terrific, but that wasn't the draw. It was the memories, always the memories—and a need that wouldn't quit. During the years they'd been apart, he'd managed to convince himself he was over her. Yet from the second he'd wrestled her to the ground at the fishing camp, his attraction to her had been almost overwhelming.

He'd spent the past few days trying to deny it. Being engaged—hollow though it was—had helped. At least then he'd had loyalty to Celeste to help keep his sensual stirrings at bay. Now he had no buffer between him and the intensity of his emotions.

And every cell in his brain told him that letting her back into his life would be a huge mistake. There was no reason to think she still felt anything for him. And even if she did, she'd never stay with him.

Her past controlled her. And, after the news he'd just received from the private detective, Langston feared that it always would. No matter what he said or did, he'd never convince her that he could keep her and Gina safe. Who could blame her after he'd let her almost get killed on Jack's Bluff?

He patted the gun in the shoulder holster he was wearing beneath his suit coat, assuring himself that he could handle any danger that might come along tonight. His marksmanship and his experiences in the service made him as competent as any bodyguard he could have hired.

He held up his wineglass for a toast. "To better days ahead," he said. Lame, but it was the best he could come up with in his emotionally agitated state.

Trish clinked her glass with his, took a sip, then looked up at him with those big brown eyes he could have melted into. "Do you want to talk about you and Celeste?"

The question caught him off-guard. "There's not a lot to say. The engagement lasted only two weeks. We gave it a whirl. It didn't work out. I guess it's much better to find that out before the wedding than after."

"You must have thought you loved each other."

"Do you think everyone who marries is in love?"

"I think they should be."

She met his gaze, and for a second he thought her eyes were moist with tears, but it was probably only the wine reflected in them.

She barely touched her salad, but he'd finished his before she took up the conversation again. "You may as well tell me about the phone call you had when we were leaving Phil Caruthers's office. I could tell it was bad news, which probably means it concerned me."

"We could talk about after we've eaten."

"I'd rather get it over with. I feel like I'm waiting for the proverbial second shoe to drop."

And he was going to have to drop it on her head. "You know that I've hired a private investigator."

"You said. Was there more news about Buck Rivers?"

"No. This time the info concerns Carlos Carletti."

"What about him?"

"Carletti is originally from Chicago. He moved away right after you and your father did."

The fork slipped from her fingers and clattered against the plate. "So, I was right. The far-reaching arm of my father's 'family' has found me again. Is there more?"

"Some. Carlos's father went to prison after the major crackdown resulting from your father's revelations to the FBI. His attorney was working on his appeal when he was killed, shot in an altercation with some other prisoners."

"And what about our Mr. Carletti?"

"He's been busy pursuing his own interests and acquiring a small fortune. He joined up with some controversial investors in opening various nightclubs across the country, including the one where Buck Rivers worked as bouncer. Caruthers nailed that one."

"No matter how long or how far I run, it never stops coming at me."

"It can," Langston said, "if things are taken care of properly."

"Maybe for people like the Collingsworths, Langston. Not for me." She took a long, slow sip of her wine. "Caruthers mentioned a gambling scandal. Did you find out more about that?"

"Carletti was accused of bribing New Orleans officials to obtain a license for poker slots in a gentleman's club he was trying to open there. The charges were dropped after the evidence against him was reported lost during Katrina or its aftermath."

"So now, twenty-eight years after the fact, he comes after me. I just don't get it. How could he possibly spend all those years looking for someone to punish for his father's death."

"My guess, the P.I.'s and Aidan's, is that he didn't.

He likely stumbled across you when his daughter brought him into your boutique, though I can't imagine how he would have recognized you."

"He recognized me the same way you knew Gina was my daughter. I look just like my mother, from the few photos I have of her. I'm sure Carletti had me investigated the same as you did, and found out that I'm not who I claim to be. I guess it isn't that hard. When did you talk to Aidan about all this? Your call in the car was only a minute or two."

"While you were in the ladies room. I tried to call Caruthers, too, but ended up leaving a message on his cell phone."

"I guess you called to tell him he was right about Carletti having ties to the old 'family.'"

"No. I called to tell him he was wrong. There is absolutely no evidence to suggest that Carlos Carletti has ever reconnected with organized crime. His branch of the family was kicked out years ago. Like the Justice Department told you, the players, especially the ones at the top, have changed several times since your grandfather's day."

"Is that supposed to make me feel better?"

"I hoped it would. It means that Carletti's working on his own. Once we prove his involvement in Selena's murder and the attack on you, then he'll go to prison, and the danger will be over."

Finally, she met his gaze, and her eyes were shadowed with defeat. So was her voice. "Just a loose cannon," she said, "just like the man who shot at my father. You never know when they'll show up. The problem is that even a loose cannon can kill you."

"WHAT WAS MY TIME?" GINA CALLED as she rode Candy over to where Trish and a half-dozen Collingsworths sat on the fence surrounding the practice arena. Zach had set up three barrels, and Gina was racing around them in the cloverleaf pattern used in rodeo competition.

Jaime checked her stopwatch. "Two-tenths of a second faster than last time. Keep that up and you'll be racing in the Colts Run Cross Rodeo by fall."

"Yee-haw," Zach called teasingly as he tipped his hat to Gina's success.

"But you have to learn to keep your head up and your hat on," Bart said. "Some rodeos fine you if your hat falls off during barrel-racing competition."

Gina frowned. "You're kidding, right?"

"No, barrel racing's about looking good," Zach said. "That's the event with the best-looking ladies."

"Which is why I used to ride in it," Jaime said.

"Mom, we have to buy me a hat that fits," Gina said. "This one of Jaime's is too big."

"See," Zach teased as he put an arm around his twin's shoulder. "Even Gina knows you've got a big head."

Jaime promptly shoved Zach off the fence.

Bart handed Gina the fallen hat he'd retrieved. She took it, but instead of retuning it to her head, she started waving it in the air. "Langston, come see me ride," she called excitedly. "I'm practicing for the rodeo."

Trish turned to see Langston striding toward them, grinning and waving back at Gina as if none of them had a problem in the world. It did almost seem that way today with the sunshine and laughter and Gina's excitement atop it all.

The Collingsworths were amazing. They had every

reason to resent that their safe, peaceful ranch was now inundated with strangers riding security details, and that the wrangler they treated like family was in the hospital recovering from a bullet wound he'd received while trying to protect Trish. Yet here they were, all spending the better part of their Saturday afternoon helping keep Gina's mind off Selena's death and the ongoing problems.

Gina had Jaime reset the stopwatch, and she did another run. She was nowhere near competition ready, but you'd never know it by the cheers of her spectators.

When she finished, she rode up to Langston. "How'd I do?"

He gave her two thumbs up. "Looking good."

Trish tried to blink back the tears that welled in her eyes. This was how it should always be for Gina. Laughing. Carefree. Safe. It was the one thing Trish could no longer give her—at least not as long as she stayed in this country. There would always be the chance they could run into someone with a murderous grudge that had been nurtured for years.

Her gaze went back to Langston and Gina. He was pointing to the barrels and talking, obviously giving pointers to his attentive listener. Trish's chest constricted. The two people she loved most in life—and she'd been doomed from the very beginning to fail both of them. The tears started to fall, and she walked away from the sunshine and laughter before Gina caught her crying.

LENORA WATCHED TRISH WALK AWAY. A minute ago she'd been laughing with the rest of them, but then

Langston had shown up and Trish had seemingly dissolved. Lenora was almost certain she was crying now.

But she'd seen the way Trish had looked at Langston when he'd first approached. As far as Lenora was concerned, the truth was indisputable. Trish Cantrell had never stopped loving her son.

Gina dismounted. The practice session was obviously over for the day. Lenora waited until Gina was walking alone, leading her horse back to the stable. She caught up with her quickly.

"I enjoyed watching you ride. You reminded me of Jaime when she was your age."

"Do you think I can come back and ride even after we go home to Dallas?"

"I'd like that a lot," Lenora said. "How old are you exactly?"

"Fifteen."

"When's your birthday?"

"March 7."

Lenora put her arm around Gina's shoulder. Now it was her eyes that welled with tears. *Fifteen.* "I'll make certain that you come back to Jack's Bluff as often as you'd like."

LANGSTON WENT LOOKING FOR TRISH the second he realized she was no longer with his family at the practice arena. She couldn't have gone far, and he was almost certain she hadn't gone back to the house. She'd have had to walk right past him to do that.

Finally, he spotted her sitting on a swing that hung from the limb of a giant oak. Her head was down, the toes of her shoes making circles in the dirt beneath her feet. His heart skipped a couple of beats. He ached to take her in his arms and hold her. That's all, just hold her close and feel her heart beating against his.

But if he did, the need raging inside him would likely erupt and he'd lose all control—the way he had sixteen years ago. He'd jumped into the physical relationship, never even thinking then about protecting his heart. He wasn't that young and impetuous now. He had the good sense to walk away, while he still could.

But he continued to watch as she brushed the back of a hand across her eyes. She was crying. Something twisted inside him, and his good intentions evaporated. He knew he'd probably regret it one day, but he couldn't bear the sight of her in tears.

In seconds he was standing in front of her and she was looking up at him, her eyes moist and soft as velvet. He opened his arms and she stepped inside them. Her tears fell on his neck and his hunger for her became slow, hot torture until he simply couldn't fight it anymore.

And then his lips were on hers, and he lost all power to reason. He kissed her until his lungs burned for air.

"Langston, we shouldn't…"

He covered her mouth with his again. He didn't want to hear excuses. He didn't want to talk of what should or shouldn't be. He didn't want to talk at all. He wanted Trish. He wanted one more perfect moment with the only woman he'd ever loved. If it ended in heartbreak, so be it. Heartbreak wouldn't kill him. She'd proven that before.

He broke from the kiss and put his lips to her ear. "Let's get out of here, Trish."

"We can't just…"

"One hour, Trish. Give me one hour. Shut out your past, the fear, the danger. Shut out everything but you and me for one hour. That's all I'm asking."

"Where will we go?"

"To the swimming hole." They both said it at once, and when she laughed, the years melted away and they were nineteen again, wild and ready for anything that might come.

"Let's take a vehicle," he said, leading her back toward the house. "I don't want to waste time saddling horses."

There was no one in sight when they reached the back driveway, and Matt's keys were dangling from the ignition of his extended cab pickup. They jumped in and Langston grabbed the clipboard and work gloves Matt had left in the passenger seat and sent them sailing to the seat behind him.

The engine roared to life at a touch and Langston swerved past the other cars and onto the dirt road that cut through the brush and off to the east. Langston didn't talk. He was afraid of conversation, scared that words would lead to Trish's changing her mind.

That was the one thing he couldn't face today.

TRISH WAS ALL TOO AWARE THAT nothing had changed. Her past still dictated her future. But an hour of Langston was more than she'd ever expected to know again. She'd grab it and make the memory last a lifetime.

Langston left the dirt road and took off across the grassy terrain, swerving his way through the scrubby underbrush. Finally he stopped the truck in the shade of the oak tree. She climbed out of the car and kicked off her sandals as Langston rounded the truck and pulled her back into his arms.

"We could swim first," she said.

"Not on my hour."

He kissed her hard on the mouth, and she reeled with the thrill of it. She kissed him back over and over, losing her breath but still not willing to pull away for more than a second. He tugged her to the soft carpet of grass, and they melded in a sensual tangle of arms and legs.

Langston wiggled out of his jeans and boxers, then tugged her knit blouse over her head and tossed it. Sensual sensations skipped along her nerve endings, burning here, tingling there and causing a sweet, wet ache between her thighs. Her hands roamed his back as he made quick work of getting rid of her bra and cupping his hands beneath her breasts.

"Oh, Trish. It's been so long."

"I'm here now." She unbuttoned his shirt and kissed her way down his chest to his rock-hard abdomen. He moaned in pleasure, then rolled her to her back. His mouth found each breast, kissing and sucking, until his lips left her nipples to explore the rest of her body.

She unbuttoned her shorts and pushed them over her hips. Langston took over then, slipping them down her legs and hurling them out of the way. He slipped his hand between her thighs, pushing them apart so that he could nibble and kiss her most erogenous places.

"Tell me what you want," he whispered. "Tell me how to please you."

"Take me as if you need me more than you've ever

needed anything in your life. Give me passion. Give me you."

He did, and she responded with the same fervent stroking, loving the way his body reacted to her touch. But nothing could have prepared her for the words he whispered as he took care of their protection.

"I love you, Trish. I don't want to, but I do."

Her heart pounded wildly in her chest as he thrust deeply inside her, over and over, rocking her very soul until they soared over the top in a wave of passion. Even in her dreams, it had never been like this.

She stayed in his arms, and still in the afterglow and exhaustion of spent passion, she hated that the lovemaking had ended so quickly. Hated that she had to go back to the past that would never let her be free. Tears welled in her eyes. She'd misled Langston before. She wouldn't do it again, at least not about her feelings for him.

"I love you, too, Langston," she whispered. "More than you'll ever know."

Loved him too much to let her past poison his life. They'd never have a future together. But she wasn't sorry they'd made love. She had the memories, and even her past couldn't rob her of those.

LANGSTON PUNCHED IN AIDAN'S number on his cell phone. He was not going to lose Trish again, and he couldn't stand by and wait for someone else to make the next move.

"What's up, Langston?"

"A trip to Dallas, and I could use a little advice from an expert."

"Is Trish facing more questioning?"

"No. I'm going alone. I'm planning to pay a visit to Carlos Carletti."

"That is *not* a good idea."

"It's the best idea I can come up with, actually the only one."

"What do you hope to gain by talking to him?"

"Some sense of whether or not he really is behind all of this."

"Clue me in. How do you plan to do that?"

"That's where your expertise would help. I'm thinking I'll play it straight. I'll tell him I'm a friend of Trish Cantrell's and I'm just trying to figure out if the carjacking by his bouncer led to Trish's friend getting killed."

"And you think from that you'll know if he hired Buck and later a second man to kill Trish?"

"I just need to see the man, Aidan. I need a feel for whether or not he put a contract out on Trish. I might be spinning my wheels, but I can't just do nothing. It's not my style."

"You're not doing nothing, Langston. You've hired the best attorney in the South, if not the country, to advise her and you've got the best private investigator in the business working the leads."

"I want to see the guy in person."

"You're not telling me everything."

"Okay, I plan to tell him I have a video I think he wants and see if he bites. If he does, at least we can narrow this down a bit, and we'll know for certain he's a major player."

"That's risky."

"The guy's a businessman. He won't shoot me in his house. He hires men to do the dirty work for him."

"I wouldn't want to stake my life on that, especially not going to his house alone. When are you going?"

"Now seems as good a time as any. I can fly over and be back by bedtime."

"Okay, tell you what, you need some pointers. First, don't mention Trish. Second… Oh, hell, why don't I go along and keep you company—as a friend, not a cop? Dallas is out of my jurisdiction. "

"I'll take that offer."

"I'll meet you at the Cessna. How long will it take you to get there?"

"Hour and a half, tops," Langston said.

"You got a date. But, for the record, I still say this is *not* a good idea."

But Langston figured it beat chewing his nails. And if he found out that Carletti was behind the attempt on Trish's life, he'd see him in prison or he'd see him dead. In spite of everything he could do, he might lose Trish to her fear of her past, but he would not lose her to a killer. Not as long as he had a shred of life in his body.

Hopefully, that would be past tonight.

Chapter Fourteen

They landed at the Dallas Executive Airport and picked up the luxury sedan that was waiting.

"Money talks," Aidan said. "Do you know the hassle I go through to get a rental? I have to show my driver's license, turn down ten kinds of insurance, and get lectured on what happens to the bad people who return the car with a pin-prick size dent. You just walk up and here sits a Mercedes S550. I've never even driven a Mercedes S550."

"You just don't deal with the right people," Langston said. "This is a friend's car. He has several so he always arranges for me to borrow one when I fly to Dallas."

"So what does your friend do, rob banks?"

"He sells jewelry—lots of jewelry." He tossed Aidan the keys. "Here's your chance."

"Now I'm chauffeur, too?"

"Go to work for me. You can have a Mercedes for your company car—not this model, of course. The rest of the staff would riot, but you can have a Mercedes and three weeks off a year."

"Tempting. Your offers are always tempting."

"Yet your answers are always no."

Aidan climbed behind the wheel, adjusted the seat and mirrors and then pulled into traffic. "You won't let me carry a gun and hang out with criminals."

"Some people think oil and gas executives are criminals."

"Especially now, I guess, with the prices so high at the pumps."

"It's not only the general public. I had a couple of visitors from the CIA yesterday."

"To what do you owe that honor?"

"They received a tip from a 'reliable' source that Collingsworth Oil is investing in terrorist activities in the Middle East."

"Did they name the source?"

"They said they weren't at liberty to do that."

"Probably some sheikh you wouldn't buy oil from. I wouldn't worry. If they had something on you, they'd say it up front. They're probably just covering their bases."

"That's what I figured. But we have a lot of employees, and I'd hate to think that any one of them had any ties to terrorists. Needless to say, I'd turn him over to the CIA in a heartbeat."

"If you're concerned about anyone, give me a call," Aidan said. "I can check them out."

"Right now I just need you to tell me how to locate the mysterious, disappearing video."

"Did you talk to the tow-truck driver?"

"Trish said Packard searched the car before it was towed."

"It never hurts to ask if they found anything. You

could call Caruthers and have him find out who did the towing. I get questions like that from attorneys all the time—usually for less reason than you have."

"Good idea." Langston pulled out his phone and punched in Caruthers's cell phone number and left a message requesting the information.

Aidan turned a corner and into what appeared to be a very exclusive gated community. He flashed his police ID, and the young man waved him through. "That's my last official duty of the night," Aidan said. "From here on out, I'm Aidan Jefferies, regular Joe." He turned at the corner. "This is the street."

Langston checked the addresses. "It should be in the next block, left side, 2437."

Aidan slowed about mid-block then pulled into a winding driveway in front of a rambling brick house that occupied the center of at least an acre of meticulously landscaped lawn. "His gardener probably drives a Mercedes," Aidan lamented as they left the car.

"And he might chase or get chased by criminals." Langston opened his car door. "What do you think goes through a man's head when he's offering someone money to take out another human being?"

"Don't ask Carletti that question. Play this cool," Aidan warned, "just the way we planned, with no mention of Trish."

The doorbell was answered by intercom. "Can I help you?"

"I'm looking for Carlos," Langston said, purposely sticking to his first name. "Is he around?"

"I think my dad's in his study. Is he expecting you?"

"No, I just took a chance he'd be in. My name's

Langston. Just tell I'm here in reference to Buck Rivers. He'll know what it's about."

"I'll check with him." In the meantime, she didn't ask them in. Smart girl. Opening doors to strangers was never a good choice.

They waited—until they heard a woman's terrified scream. Aidan forgot his own rule for the night and started banging on the door. "Police. Open the door and stand back."

He kept banging and yelling until a young woman opened the door. Langston recognized her at once as Carletti's daughter, the bride-to-be on the boutique surveillance film. Her face was pasty white, and she was shaking so hard she could barely stand on her own.

"Somebody just killed my father."

They both rushed past her, following her bloody footprints to the body. Carlos Carletti was most definitely dead.

TWO HOURS LATER, SIPPING STRONG coffee and munching on ham sandwiches and fries in a café near the airport, Langston was finally forced to admit that showing up at Carlos Carletti's house that night had not been a good idea. Shortly before they'd arrived, someone had apparently slipped into the house through an unlocked back door and slit Carletti's throat while his daughter had been watching television in the media room.

The police officers who'd arrived after the 9-1-1 call decided that by virtue of their being strangers at the scene of the crime, Aidan and Langston qualified as legitimate suspects. Had Aidan not been a cop, they'd probably both be sleeping behind bars tonight.

"Are you sure you don't want to go to work for me and give up homicide?" Langston asked.

"No way. This is the kind of stuff I get hooked on. Not the murder. That's never pretty. It's putting the pieces together and getting slime off the streets that keeps me coming back for more. But this, my friend, is one complicated puzzle."

"And getting more so by the minute."

Aidan loaded a fry with ketchup and popped it in his mouth. "Let's review what we have. Carjacking. Carjacker shot by the rescuing officer. Threatening phone call about a video, the call possibly made by rescuing officer." He picked up his sandwich. "Your turn."

Langston chewed and swallowed. "Breaking and entering of a private residence with extensive vandalism, also possibly committed by said rescuing officer. Salesgirl murdered inside a boutique. Attempted murder at Jack's Bluff Ranch."

"And tonight we had yet another murder at the home of a man who may have possibly hired a hit man to kill carjacking victim." He loaded another fry. "What have we left out?"

"Trish's past."

"And that's an overriding factor in everything. As a cop we look at motive, means and opportunity, but that's not a lot of help here until we figure out what's at the center of the mystery."

"My day requires constant prioritizing," Langston said, trying to put this in a format more familiar to him. "If I were prioritizing this, I think I'd start with the video."

"Interesting. Why the video and not the carjacking or Trish's past?"

"It was the cause that produced the effects."

"I'd say the carjacking was the trigger," Aidan countered. "It's the first event in the chain."

Langston considered Aidan's input. "But the carjacking would have been over and done with if not for the video. Woman carjacked. Perp caught and killed. End of story," Langston said. "At least that's how I see it. Second on my list would be Trish's past."

"What's your reasoning there?"

"It quite possibly relates to the motive for all our crimes."

"You're not bad at this. Maybe you should become a detective."

"I don't like chasing criminals." He dropped the conversation until the waitress who'd stopped to refill their coffee cups walked away again. "I think third in my prioritization would have to be Detective Gary Packard."

Aidan frowned. "Always the poor maligned cop. What's his ranking based on?"

"On giving credence to Trish's instincts, in the case of both the phone call and the intruder."

"Both of which could easily have been misjudgments on her part. She was under a lot of stress from the carjacking at that point." Aidan finished the last of his fries and reached for a couple of Langston's. "Based on your instincts, who do you think killed Carlos Carletti?"

"Not the daughter. She was genuinely horrified." Langston pushed back from the table. "We can theorize all night, but we won't have the answers to these questions until we have that video. I predict that once we have it, the puzzle pieces will march themselves into place."

"In the meantime we're stuck with motive, means and opportunity," Aidan said.

"Packard's stuck with it. My only responsibility is keeping Trish safe, and I definitely plan to do that."

"She's pretty big in your life right now, isn't she?"

"Christmas, New Year's and the Astros winning the World Series all rolled into one," Langston admitted. And right now he couldn't wait to get back to Jack's Bluff and hopefully make love with her all night long.

BONNEGAN'S TOWING SERVICE had three drivers, all kin and all owning their own trucks. The dispatcher was married to one of the drivers. Based on the time and location of the towing of Trish's car, the dispatcher had been able to track down the service number and tell Gary Packard the driver's name, phone number and address.

The name was Pitt Bonnegan, the address was in one of the older mobile home parks on the outskirts of town, and the phone had apparently been turned off for the evening. Gary fumed the entire forty-five-minute drive, but was relieved to find the tow truck parked at the end of a dead-end street at the back of the park, right across from Pitt's mobile home. There wasn't a neighbor for a good two hundred yards.

Gary knew this was less than a long shot. He had checked the scene too well for there to have been a slipup. His visit tonight was insurance against Phil Caruthers's coming out here and instigating trouble. He wouldn't put that kind of antic past him, especially after he'd called tonight wanting additional information about the towing.

He knocked on the door. No one answered, but he

could hear the TV blaring inside. He banged repeatedly until he got a response. The man who opened the door was wearing a pair of baggy shorts and a grease-stained T-shirt. He reeked of garlic and marijuana.

Gary could arrest him on drug charges, but he wouldn't. The guy was home and not bothering anyone. He flashed his ID and explained the situation.

"I don't ever look in the cars I tow," Pitt said, slurring his words. "It's against the rules."

"I realize that. I'm just asking if you picked up a video or anything else from around this particular car when you moved it."

"I can't remember every car I tow, but I haven't picked up a video. I just go to the site and tow the car. That's it, officer. I follow the rules."

An ironic claim with the odor of pot all around them.

"You're not planning to drive that tow truck any-where tonight, are you?"

"No, sir. I'm off tonight. I'm not going nowhere."

"Okay, buddy, see that you don't. You're in no shape to drive."

Gary drove back to the city and was walking the block to his favorite club when he got a call from one of the other homicide cops. "Yo."

"Gary, all right, man, I was hoping I could catch you before you fell into bed with a big-breasted blonde for a Saturday night boogie."

"What's up?"

"Same old, same old. Another murder. You might be interested in this one, though. It could be connected to that Hernandez case you're working on."

He swallowed a curse. He didn't need another

murder. He needed an arrest, and he was just on the verge of getting it. "What's the tie-in?"

"Carlos Carletti was murdered in his home tonight, but get this. Two men from Houston showed up at his house even before the daughter had found the body. When they got there they told the daughter they wanted to see Carlos about Buck Rivers."

"Who were the men?"

"I don't have the details, but one was a Houston detective—off duty. I'll keep you posted."

"Yeah, do that."

"And let me have a look at what you get on handprints ASAP."

He'd been wrong. This could be a hell of a connection. Sam Little was as good as convicted.

PITT STAGGERED BACK TO HIS recliner and plopped down in front of the TV. He was weak with relief. He'd dodged a bullet that time. That dumb cop wouldn't know a reefer if it jumped up and bit him. But that must have been some video that fell out of the wrecked car if he came all the way out here looking for it.

Pitt remembered the video. He'd spotted it in the ditch underneath the car. It was covered in mud, and he just figured it was trash someone threw out of their car when they drove by. The only reason he'd bothered to pick it up and wipe it off was because it was unlabeled and he figured it was probably porn.

He would have looked for it except that he couldn't let the cop come in with his stash of pot lying out in the open. Besides, it might have taken hours to find the video in this mess.

You know, come to think of it, he might have left that old video in his truck. He'd go check. He could use some good porn tonight.

He found it in the side pocket of the passenger side door, took it in, wiped it off with a damp cloth and stuck in the VCR player.

It surprised him when the thing started playing. "What the…" He muttered a string of curses. This wasn't porn. It was… Oh, no. This was bad. Really bad. He had to call somebody.

But not tonight. He'd had too much to smoke. But first thing in the morning, he was calling the FBI.

IT WAS PAST MIDNIGHT AND THE big house was dark when Langston finally put his key in the lock and opened the door. He was tired, but still he was considering grabbing a shower and knocking on Trish's bedroom door. Making love with her this afternoon had changed his whole concept of their past relationship.

He loved her and she loved him. Whatever had happened in the years they'd been apart, whatever either of them had done, they could put it behind them and make a new life together. But only if he could convince her he could keep her safe. Somehow he had to make that happen.

He started to the kitchen for a glass of water, and then paused when he heard the television playing in the den. Either someone was sitting in the dark watching it or they'd gone to bed and left it on. He sidetracked to the den to check.

"I thought I heard you come in."

"Mom, what are you doing up so late?"

"Waiting on you. We need to talk."

"At midnight."

"It's important, Langston. It's about Trish and Gina."

She was upset, and that upped his own apprehension. He dropped into the chair across from where she sat on the sofa. "What about them?"

"I overheard Matt and Bart talking. Matt said that Trish will have to go on the run again. When I confronted him, he said I should talk to you."

"Don't worry about it, Mom. It's all going to work out."

"Don't patronize me, Langston. I want an honest explanation."

"Trish's father testified against the Mafia years ago," he said, determined to keep this simple. "He and Trish went into protective custody for a while, but that ended before Trish and I met. She thinks her present problems could be related to that, but there's no proof of it at this point."

"Why didn't you tell me about this?"

"I didn't want to worry you unnecessarily."

"I am worried. You can't let Trish leave, Langston. You can't let her run with Gina."

So that's what this was about. Langston leaned forward and rested his elbows on his knees. "I know you're fond of Gina, Mother. We all are, and believe me, I'm doing everything in my power to make sure both she and Trish are safe. I'll keep doing that, but in the end it will be Trish's decision whether she goes or stays."

"And Gina? What will happen to her?"

"She's Trish's daughter. If Trish leaves, I'm sure she'll take her with her. I have no control over that."

"Go upstairs and talk to Trish, Langston. Demand she tell you about Gina's father."

"Calm, down, Mother. It's after midnight, and…"

"And the truth is sixteen years past due, Langston."

He was missing something here. "What are you saying?"

"Gina will be *sixteen* next March, Langston. *Early* March."

Early March. Nine months from the time Trish had walked out on him. How could he have been so blind?

He stormed out of the room and up the stairs. This time he didn't bother to knock on Trish's door. He shoved it open and stepped inside.

Chapter Fifteen

Trish jerked to a sitting position as Langston stepped into her bedroom, his hard, drawn features highlighted in the moonlight streaming through the window. "Langston, what's wrong?"

"Tell me about Gina's father."

Her heart slammed against her chest, and she yanked the sheet up to her neck as if that could protect her from the venom in his voice. "Why?"

He walked to the foot of her bed. "Tell me about him."

"There's nothing to tell. He's just a man I met right after we escaped to London. I got pregnant with Gina and he died before we could get married."

"You were on the Pill."

"I forgot to get it refilled. I was on the run."

He jerked the sheet from her hands and threw it the foot of the bed. "Let's get everything out in the open, Trish. No more lies. I want to know now! Is Gina my daughter?"

She scooted away from him until her back was up against the headboard. Her insides were shaking so badly she could barely think.

Langston moved to the side of the bed and sat down

beside her, so close that even in the moonlight she could see the anger burning in his dark eyes. "Is Gina my daughter?" he demanded again.

This wasn't how this moment was supposed to be. But, like all of her life, everything came with a killer price.

"Yes." The answer came out as a shaky whisper, and she wasn't even sure Langston had heard it until she saw his muscles flex and his body go rigid.

"How could you do this? How in God's name could you ever steal the first fifteen years of my daughter's life from me?"

He turned away as if he couldn't bear to look at her now. The love that had filled her heart just hours before spilled out, leaving her heart a shriveled, painful lump.

"I had to do it, Langston. I had to do it to keep her safe."

His hands knotted into fists. "That was my job as much as yours, Trish. I'm her father. I should have been in on those decisions. You should have told me you were pregnant with my child."

"If I had, you would never have let me take her away from you."

"So *you* took her away from *me* instead." He stood and paced the room. Finally he stopped at the bed again, this time wrapping his hand around the bedpost as he stared down at her. "My daughter is fifteen years old, Trish. Fifteen, and we're basically strangers."

There was agony in his voice now, and it hurt even more than his anger. "It wasn't what I wanted, Langston. It was the way it had to be. If you'd known about her, you would have used your money and clout to take her away from me."

"You're wrong, Trish. I would have made certain

she was safe, but I would have never kept her from you the way you kept her from me."

"Can't you at least try to understand? I did what I had to do to keep her safe. I couldn't lose her to a killer the way I lost my mother and baby brother. I couldn't."

"I understand a lot, Trish. I understand that I wasn't there to hold my daughter in my arms when she was born. I missed her first smile, her first steps, her first words. I never got to tell her a bedtime story or comfort her when she'd had a bad dream." His voice broke. "How would you feel if someone had taken that from you?"

"Please, don't do this, Langston. Don't do it to me. Don't do it to us."

"Why didn't you come to me and tell me I had a daughter when you moved back to Dallas?"

"I thought about it a million times, but always in the back of my mind I knew that the day would come when I'd have to run again. And…"

"No use in holding back, Trish."

"Your family is too prominent. You're the Collingsworths of Texas. There is no way to go unnoticed as your daughter. Someone would have eventually figured out that Gina was a Lombardio, too."

"I could have kept our daughter safe."

"The way you kept me safe when someone shot at me the other day on Jack's Bluff?"

She was sorry the second the words left her mouth. He didn't deserve that, but she didn't deserve the condemnation he'd been hurling at her, either.

Langston jumped to his feet, his back ramrod straight. "If you think I can't protect you, you're free to leave."

"I didn't mean that. Please, Langston, try to understand."

"I understand that Gina is my daughter. She's a Collingsworth, and she will always have a place in this family. The only question now is would you like to tell her, or shall I?"

Trish choked back her tears. This was all so wrong, so horribly wrong. "I'll tell her tomorrow."

"Let me know when it's done."

He turned and left, closing the door behind him. She fell back to the bed and let her heart finish breaking as sobs shook her body and tears ran hot on her pillow. She loved Langston with all her heart. She always had. She always would. She'd never meant to hurt him.

But if it meant keeping Gina safe, she'd do it all over again.

TRISH SPENT A SLEEPLESS NIGHT, much of it in tears. By morning her eyes were red and swollen. She went to the bathroom, grabbed a cold shower and patted her face dry. The only makeup she had with her were the touch-up items she'd had in her purse when she'd escaped from her house a few nights ago.

A few nights. A lifetime.

She dabbed a bit of tinted moisturizer over the dark circles. The tint made no noticeable difference.

What she could really use was a cup of coffee, but she wasn't willing to risk running into Langston to get it. She wasn't too keen on seeing the rest of the Collingsworths, either. It was likely they all knew the truth by now. Everyone knew except Gina.

Trish would remedy that this morning. Gina would

be shocked to find out that her father was not only alive, but here with them. Trish had spent half the night trying to gauge the rest of her daughter's reaction to the reason Trish had kept her from her father all these years. She prayed it would not be as condemning as Langston's had been.

The smell of frying bacon merged with the odor of fresh-brewed coffee, all of it wafting up the stairs and beneath her closed door. The Collingsworth Sunday breakfast.

Trish had forgotten about that tradition, though she'd joined in one once before. The table had been crowded with delicious, rich foods that the Collingsworths had somehow managed to devour though they'd all been talking and laughing at once. After cleanup, Lenora and everyone she could persuade to go with her left for church. She and Langston had stayed behind, hoping for time alone. That was before they'd made love, but not before they'd fallen hard for each other.

"Mom, you better hurry. You'll miss breakfast."

"I'm not hungry this morning."

"But Juanita's off on Sundays, and you should see the food Mrs. Collingsworth cooked. Awesome. And there are fresh peaches and blueberry muffins that she baked herself."

"It sounds wonderful, but I'm not dressed yet."

"Are you sick? 'Cause your eyes are all puffy."

"Just a little trouble with my sinuses. I'll be fine. You go on down and enjoy breakfast, and when you're finished, come back up. I'd like to talk over some things with you."

"Okay, I'll tell everybody you're not feeling well. Do

you want me to bring you a plate of food when I come back?"

"No, but coffee would be good."

"I'll get that for you."

Gina bounded down the stairs and returned a few minutes later carrying a wooden tray overflowing with coffee and food.

"How thoughtful," Trish said, when Gina sat the tray on the round table beneath the window.

"Mrs. Collingsworth fixed it for you. She said she hoped you felt better real soon. She's nice, huh?"

"Very nice." And the nice Mrs. Collingsworth would have a new granddaughter by the time she returned from church. Gina would be a Collingsworth, part of a boisterous, energetic, loving Texas family with roots to forever and back again.

The perfect life—as long as there were no loose cannons or Carlos Carlettis about.

DETECTIVE GARY PACKARD was standing at his desk, smiling and looking over the evidence spread across his desk when the chief of police walked in. He crossed the room, extended one hand for shaking and clapped Gary on the back with the other.

"Good work, Packard. This is the way I like to start a week."

"We lucked out with the fingerprints," Gary said. "If we hadn't, I don't how we'd have tied Sam Little to the crime. All we had before was proof that he'd been in the Cottage Boutique on several occasions."

"What about motive?"

"I hope to know more after we get the warrant and

bring him in for questioning, but right now I'd say Buck Rivers was back to his old tricks, if he ever left them. He just thought he was too smart to get caught."

The chief screwed up his face, making his mustache look as if it might crawl into his nose. "I'm not following."

"Buck was suspected of doing at least a dozen hits for the Mafia before he moved to Dallas. The way it looks now is that someone paid him to take out Trish Cantrell. He abducted her to kill her, only it backfired and I took him out."

"One less murdering lunatic we have to take to trial—and don't say I said that."

"Said what?"

"So," the chief said, "when Buck Rivers got killed, Sam Little became the hit man du jour?"

"Right."

"And his motive?"

"He played the horses and bet every sporting event that Vegas put a line out on. The guy was buried in debt—and not to the most forgiving of people."

"Where does the video and the break-in at Trish Cantrell's home play into this?"

"I got a hunch that was just a setup to throw us off. Once Rivers screwed up the carjacking, Sam figured he could tie the murder into that and be home-free. That probably influenced his decision to take Rivers's place."

"Any idea who put out the contract on Trish to start with?"

"Not yet, but I'll keep on it. Somebody's desperate to see her dead. If we don't get him, he will get her."

"Well, all I can say is, you did it again, Gary. You're

probably responsible for getting more garbage off the streets of Dallas than the public works department."

"Just doing my job."

TRISH HAD DECIDED IT WOULD BE easier to have the formidable chat with Gina in the outdoors where they'd have total privacy. She needn't have worried. The house was empty. Evidently the Collingsworths had gone to church en masse this morning—minus Langston— probably at the insistence of Lenora, who would have wanted them out of the way. She had a feeling Lenora had counted the months between her departure and Gina's birth, too. Or else Langston had told her.

Langston was in the stables. He'd told Trish he'd be there when Gina was ready to talk to him. They were the only words he'd said to her since he'd stormed out of her room last night.

"Let's sit in the shade," Trish said, stopping near one of the large oaks behind the house.

"Okay." Gina plopped to the ground and crossed her legs. "This is about Selena's killer, isn't it?"

"No, why do you think that?"

"You're acting funny. Not ha-ha funny but like you're about to tell me something that's going to upset me."

She was obviously handling this all wrong. Trish leaned against the trunk of the tree and stretched her legs out in front of her. "I do have something to tell you that's going to surprise you, but it's a nice surprise. It's about your father."

"He's dead. What kind of surprise can be about him?"

"Actually, he's not dead." This wasn't getting easier.

She had to just get this out and go from there. "Langston Collingsworth is your father."

Gina looked at her mother as if she had two heads. "Is this some kind of joke, like April Fools in July?"

"It's not a joke, Gina. Langston and I were more than friends. We fell in love that summer before your grandfather and I moved to London. I got pregnant and you were born the next March."

Gina stared at Trish accusingly. "Why are you saying this? My father's dead. He was killed in a car wreck. I have the newspaper clipping about it. You gave it to me."

"The man in that wreck wasn't your father. I didn't even know that man. I just saw the article in the paper and made the rest up."

"I don't understand."

"I know you don't, sweetheart. I just hope that when you hear it all, you'll realize that I did what I had to do." It was time to tell Gina the whole story.

Gina interrupted with dozens of questions as Trish explained everything from the time she'd gone on the run with her parents and baby brother the day after her seventh birthday to her life since Gina was born. She left nothing out, although she tried to keep the gore and the horror to a minimum.

She'd always planned to tell Gina the truth one day, just not like this. Not when her own heart was breaking. And not when they were still in danger.

"Does Langston know that I'm his daughter?"

"He figured it out and confronted me with it last night. I admitted everything."

"Who else knows?"

"I'm not sure. All the Collingsworths will know soon. It's not a secret any longer."

Gina had stopped sitting about midway through the explanation. Now she dropped back to the ground beside Trish. She picked up a twig and rolled it between her palms. "So what does this mean? Will we live here at Jack's Bluff? Will you and Langston get married?"

Tears welled in Trish's eyes and she turned away, hoping Gina wouldn't notice. "Our life will be like before. We'll go back to Dallas as soon as it's safe, and you can visit the ranch summers and some weekends."

"But what about you? Don't you like it here?"

"Yeah. I like it here, but you're the Collingsworth, not me. Don't worry, Gina. It's all going to work out. I know Langston would like to see you. He's in the stables."

"Will you go with me?"

"Sure."

They walked hand in hand. It took a few seconds for Trish's eyes to adjust to the dimness of the stables after being in the bright sunshine. When they did, she saw Langston leaning against a stall gate. He was dressed in jeans, a white Western shirt, his boots and his Stetson. Every inch a cowboy, and so gorgeous he took her breath away.

Trish managed a smile as she nodded to tell him that the talk was over. Gina took a step toward him, then stopped and looked back at Trish. "Go say hello to your dad," she whispered. "You'll love him. There's no way not to."

Tears ran down Trish's cheeks as she dropped back into the shadows and watched the first tentative exchange between Langston and Gina. And then he put his arms around her and they embraced. It was a moment dreams are made of. Except if this were really a dream, Trish would be with them instead of walking away alone.

LANGSTON HAD DRIVEN INTO WORK Monday morning for a nine o'clock meeting to hear reports on the feasibility of a new wave of exploratory drilling in the Gulf of Mexico. He'd been glad for the excuse to get away from the ranch, but now that he was at the office, he was finding it incredibly difficult to concentrate on business.

Sunday with Gina had gone well, although there had been some awkward moments as they tried to fit into the unfamiliar relationship. She was terrific. Smart, sensitive, with remarkable verve. So much like her mother.

Things would be fine between him and Gina. Trish was the problem. He couldn't forgive her for waiting so long to tell him he had a child, yet he couldn't get her out of his mind. If he hadn't held her in his arms... hadn't kissed her...hadn't made love with her.

His phone vibrated. He pulled it from his pocket and checked the caller ID. Phil Caruthers. He stood, slipped out of the conference room and took the call.

"Good news," Caruthers said as soon as he'd answered.

"I could use that. Did you find out the name of the towing company?"

"I did. It's Bonnegan's, and the driver who towed Trish's car was Pitt Bonnegan. But I have better news that than. The DPD has made an arrest in Selena's murder case."

"Whom did they arrest?"

"Remember the man you noticed in the picture, the one you said came in with Buck Rivers?"

"I remember."

"His name is Sam Little, and he's a bartender at the same club where Rivers worked. His fingerprints were found both in Trish's home and in the office where Selena Hernandez was murdered."

Langston listened while Caruthers filled him in on the details, including the fact that Detective Packard claimed to have evidence that Little had also killed Carletti. It sounded almost too good to be true.

"We have just one little problem," Caruthers said.

"If we're down to one, we're miles ahead of where we were. What is it?"

"Since Trish went into hiding after her house was broken into, she never actually filed a complaint with the police. They need it to complete the paperwork."

"What does she need to do?"

"Gary Packard wants her to come in, this afternoon, if possible. I've got to be in court, but I told him I'd see if she wanted to go in without me."

"No problem. I'll fly her to Dallas. We should be there by two."

"I'll pass that word along."

Langston was torn with mixed emotions as he broke the connection. With Carletti dead and Sam Little in jail, the danger might all be over. Trish and Gina would go back to Dallas. He'd go back to living in the penthouse with maybe every other weekend with the daughter he barely knew, and with no time with Trish.

But there would be plenty of time to worry about that later—like for the rest of his life.

LANGSTON STOOD OFF TO THE SIDE as Trish signed the required paperwork for Detective Packard. It was the first time he'd met the man, but he didn't like him. He had that fake friendliness about him that Langston never trusted. And Trish had thought he'd broken into her home hadn't she? But then who *did* he trust these days?

"I guess that about does it." Detective Packard shook Langston's hand and then turned back to Trish.

"I'm really sorry you had to go through all this, Ms. Cantrell. I wish we could have gotten Sam Little and Buck Rivers off the streets before Selena Hernandez was murdered."

"Me, too."

"I may need to get in touch with you again. Are you going to stick around Dallas for a while?"

"Yes. I'll be here, at least until I can sell the boutique. I've kind of lost my taste for that shop."

"I can't say that I blame you. So what will you do now?"

"I'm catching a taxi when I leave here and going home to start cleaning up. From what I've heard about the condition Sam Little left it in, that may take me quite awhile."

"But you gotta remember that the mess led to definite fingerprints."

"Fingerprints aren't necessarily enough to assure a conviction, are they?" Langston asked. "Couldn't a good attorney still get him off?"

"A good attorney? I better not say what we cops call an attorney who puts criminals back on the street." He gathered the paperwork he had spread on his desk and stuffed it all back into a manila folder. "I've signed the release on your car, Trish. You can have it towed to a garage for repair anytime."

"Thanks. I have to decide whether to have it fixed or buy a new one. As it stands now, I left the rental I had out of town when I fled my house."

"I'll have someone pick that up and bring it to you," Langston offered.

"I'll take care of it," she said, making it clear she didn't need his help.

"I can give you a lift to one of the downtown rental agencies," Packard offered. "I have to take care of some business in that area anyway as soon as I hand this to the records clerk."

"That would be great."

"You got it. Be right back."

Langston waited until the helpful detective had walked away. He hated that things had become so awkward between him and Trish. "Are you sure you don't want me to have the car picked up from the camp?"

"I'm sure, Langston. You've done more than enough, and I am capable of taking care of myself."

"I know that. At least let me drive you to the car rental agency."

"The detective's going that way. Besides, you must have a million things to take care of at Collingsworth Oil after being away for most of a week. And you have Gina—until Sunday."

"Thanks for letting her stay. I'll fly her home."

"Fine."

"I don't want our relationship to become like this. I'm trying to understand your reasons for…"

She turned and locked her gaze with his. "But you

don't understand. You can't understand unless you've stood there and watched someone you love with all your being shot so full of holes that your father has to scrape them off the floor like raw meat."

Her voice shook with emotion and tears welled in her eyes. He reached out to her but she jerked away from him.

"Okay," Packard said, joining them again. "Ready to roll."

"I'm ready," Trish said. She didn't give Langston a backward glance as she walked away.

He had to force himself not to run after her. He wanted to just pick her up and carry her back to Jack's Bluff. But there had been too many lies over a period of too many years. Too much time that he'd lost with Gina. Time he could never make up. He just didn't see how he could ever get past all of that and make it work with Trish. Especially when he knew that she could run again at any time.

GARY PACKARD MADE THE TURN out of the DPD parking lot. "What do you think about Phil Caruthers?"

"He seems very competent," Trish said.

"Criminal defense attorneys like him are one of the reasons that crime in Texas is soaring. In the old days, cops could get the criminals off the streets. Now those high-powered attorneys and know-it-all judges put them right back out there faster than we can make the arrests.

"Take a man like Carlos Carletti. There is no way a rich bastard like that would have ever served a day in prison. Even if he was convicted by a jury, there would have been appeal after appeal until he got off."

"I guess."

"No guessing about it. Dead is the only way the system works anymore."

The conversation made her edgy, and she was thankful when they reached the rental agency and she could tell Packard goodbye for what she hoped was the last time. Still, when she got out of the car, she couldn't help but remember how certain she'd been that he was her intruder.

LANGSTON HEADED TOWARD HIS borrowed car for the drive back to the airport. It had been a hell of a week. It was a good thing he wasn't a detective. He'd still be looking for a video and probably on his way to talk to Pitt Bonnegan right now.

He'd been so sure the video had played a major role in the mystery. Sam Little had gone to a lot of trouble to perpetrate the ruse. And it still didn't all add up.

Langston could see the phone call and the damage to Trish's house as a ruse, but the search at the boutique still puzzled him. His first thoughts on it still seemed to make more sense. The house had been searched hurriedly. Sam probably thought Trish had gone to call the police, and he had to finish before they showed up. He had more time at the shop so he searched methodically. Only there was no need to do that if the search were only a ruse.

Bonnegan's Towing Service.

The name almost taunted him as he drove to the airport. Packard was probably right that there had never been a video, but how much trouble could one phone call be?

A lot, he found out. He went through directory assistance and the dispatcher at Bonnegan's Towing Service before he finally got Pitt Bonnegan on the phone. He decided on the positive approach.

"I'm calling about a video that you found on a towing job."

"You must be with the FBI."

The word "no" was almost out of his mouth when Langston changed his answer to "Right, the FBI. About that video…"

TRISH GOT OUT OF THE COMPACT car she'd just rented, closed the garage and unlocked the door to the laundry room. It was good to be home. She dropped her keys and handbag to the counter by the door and turned the heavy double bolts.

They were locked tight before her gaze fell on the open toolbox. Memories of the last time she'd walked into the house flooded her mind. Her nerves grew jumpy. She took a deep breath and tried to settle them.

Buck Rivers and Carlos Carletti were dead, and Sam Little was in jail. The danger was past.

"Welcome home, Trish."

Her heart flew to her throat. "Detective. What are you doing here?"

"I came for the video."

Instinctively, she lunged for the toolbox and anything she could use as a weapon. Packard grabbed her arm before she could reach it and twisted it behind her back until the pain made her cry out.

"You're not a fighter, Trish. You don't have the stomach for it. If you had, you would have put my eye out with the screwdriver last time I was here instead of missing your mark altogether." He pushed a shock of hair from his forehead.

She saw the wound now, a jagged scratch that had been hidden before. "It was enough to slow you down."

"Where's the video?"

"I don't have a video, detective. I've never had it. I don't even know what you're talking about."

He shoved her to the floor and kicked her in the head so hard that her brain seemed to rattle in her scull. She hadn't seen the pistol before, but it was in his right hand now and pointing right at her. He was going to kill her over a video that she didn't have. She had to think, had to find a way to convince him that she didn't know anything.

"I never saw a video. I promise you that."

"Do you think I would be here now if I hadn't seen Buck Rivers get into your car that day with the video in his hands?"

"But you weren't there when Buck carjacked me."

"Oh, I was there, all right, I was supposed to meet him so he could collect his blackmail money. But it didn't work that way because smart cops don't reward scum like Buck Rivers. I might even have gone on believing you were a random victim as you claimed if you'd handed me the video that day instead of holding on to it."

"I don't know what you're talking about."

"Sure you do. You knew Buck. You and that slut Selena both knew him. You might as well admit it. You knew about the video and you thought you could black-mail me with it when things cooled down. Too bad you'll never live to do it."

So the carjacking had been random in a way. Buck had been parked outside the restaurant to meet Packard. When the detective hadn't shown up and she had, Buck had decided it was the perfect time to make his hit on her. He would have killed her on that deserted road if Packard hadn't been following them.

She tried to scoot away from him. He kicked her again, this time in the stomach. She retched and fought not to throw up. "Go ahead and kill me. But it won't help. Buck must have backup copies of the video."

"And do you think I'm so stupid that I don't have them all in my possession? Nice thing about dead scum. They don't get in your way when you break into their houses."

Things got suddenly clearer. "You killed Buck on purpose. You must have killed Carletti, too. And Selena. You killed them all. It wasn't Sam Little. It was you."

"Sam is scum."

"Selena wasn't." Fury swallowed her fear, and she kicked at his legs, causing him to stumble toward the door. Hot pain shot through her stomach and head as she jumped to her feet and ran into the hall. She was almost to the front door before he caught her by the hair and threw her against the wall.

"Forget the video, Trish. I'll find it on my own. Like I said, dead people never get in the way."

Oh, God, this was it. She was going to die at the hands of a mad cop. She'd never get to tell Gina goodbye. What if Gina didn't have Langston? What if Trish had died, and Gina had been left all alone?

Langston had been right. She'd let her fear of her past rob them all of so much. Loose cannons could never be predicted. They had to be fought one battle at a time.

She lunged at Packard as the sound of gunfire clattered through her brain.

Take care of Gina, Langston. I love you both so very much.

Chapter Sixteen

"It's okay, Trish. It's okay. I'm here."

For a second she wasn't sure if she was dreaming or dead. "Langston?"

"Right, baby. I'm right here with you. Are you okay?"

"The detective…"

"I know. You had him pegged from the get-go."

She scanned the room, although she was so woozy from the kick to the head it took a few seconds to spot the detective. He was lying on the floor with two uniformed police officers standing over him. Even with blood soaking his shirt he was still muttering about getting scum off the streets of Dallas.

"I thought I'd been shot, but the police shot him."

"No," Langston said. "I did. The police arrived a second too late."

"I love you, Langston. And you were right. I should have told you about Gina long ago."

He cradled her aching head in his arms. "We were both right. I never knew fear the way I did when I saw that gun pointing at your head."

Langston kissed the top of her head. "Your face is all swollen."

"He kicked me hard."

"I'm sorry. Is there anything I can get you?"

"Just hold me."

"I plan to. I plan to hold on to you for the rest of my life."

"One other thing. How did you know to come back?"

"I have the video."

Epilogue

One month later

"How did I do?"

"You just beat your best time by three tenths of a second."

"You got it going, cowgirl."

"You didn't even lose your hat that time."

Lenora stood in the shade watching the action in the practice arena. It was almost sundown, but still hot. It always was in South Texas in August. The rest of the family was either leaning on, hanging on or perched on the wooden fence, watching and applauding Gina's efforts.

Well, except for Derrick and David. Her young grandsons were chasing each and yelling like banshees. It was good to have them back at Jack's Bluff, though she'd like it better if Becky and Nick got back together.

Lenora watched as Gina rode Candy over to her parents for high fives. Langston's arm was around Trish. He couldn't keep his hands off of her, nor she him. They were so in love.

"Don't you look happier than a boardinghouse pup?"

Lenora turned at the voice. "Billy Mack, I didn't hear you walk up."

"You were too busy smiling at the new lovers."

"I do like seeing Langston so happy."

"And you got a granddaughter in the deal."

"A terrific granddaughter, though I won't get to see as much of her after she starts back to school in Dallas next week. And I absolutely adore Trish. She's had so much to deal with and still grieving for her friend, Selena, but she's a blessing to have around. Life is good, Billy Mack. Life is really good."

"I can tell that just by looking at you. So when's the wedding?"

"I wish I knew. I've asked Langston what he's waiting for. All he says is that they have issues to work out. But I know they're in love and that's what matters. The rest will come in time."

"Any more news about what's going on with Gary Packard?"

"Yes," Lenora said. "That question I can answer since Langston's still keeping up with everything. Detective Packard's in jail and going to stand trial for killing Selena. And, with the video Langston recovered that shows him kicking and beating to death the unarmed man outside that club where Buck Rivers worked, he'll face charges for that, too. Not to mention that he planted the fingerprint evidence against Sam Little."

"But it was Sam who shot at Trish here on the ranch, wasn't it?"

"Yes, he's plea bargaining, so he not only confessed to that but also to killing Carletti. But he claims that was self defense."

"How did he explain that one?"

"He knew about the contract that was out on Trish, so when Buck Rivers was shot, he went to Carletti and offered to take his place as hit man. He chickened out after he almost got killed himself here on the ranch, so he went back to Carletti and told him he wanted out of the deal. Carletti threatened him, and he sliced the man's throat. At least that's his story.

"It all adds up. Birds of a feather don't only flock together, they sometimes run into the same storm. This time the storm was a cop who'd crossed the line."

"Whatever that means. I'll just take the old 'all's well that ends well.' Oh, and more good news. Jeremiah recognized me again today. That's five straight days in a row. I'm bringing him home from the convalescent center next week."

"I'll be by to see him."

Billy Mack went over to the fence to join the others.

Lenora walked back toward the house, stopping by the spot under the oldest oak tree where she'd buried Randolph. "Langston and Trish are perfect together. You'd be proud of him. He's really happy, and he makes a great father." She glanced back at the family gathered around the arena.

"If you're keeping score, Randolph, that makes two down and four to go. On second thought, make that one and a half and four and a half." Becky still had a way to go—Lenora had her work cut out for her.

THE SUN HAD FALLEN LOW in the sky by the time Gina gave up practice for the day. Gina headed to the stables on Candy, and the family who still remained started back to the house with David and Derrick running in front of them. Langston and Trish trailed behind.

Trish hated to see the day end and dreaded even more the long drive back to Dallas. Langston usually flew them back and forth for weekends, but he'd been out of town on business until late Friday night and Gina had begged to come up on Friday morning. She'd wanted one last long weekend at Jack's Bluff before starting back to school on Tuesday morning.

Gina had asked again today why they couldn't just move to the ranch. Trish had dodged the question. Not that she wanted to live on the ranch. She wanted to live in Houston with Langston, but he hadn't asked her to move in.

She stopped walking.

Langston took a few more steps, then turned back. "Is something the matter?"

She hesitated, then took a deep breath and blurted out her frustrations. "I need to know where we stand, Langston. Are you still angry with me for not telling you sooner that you had a daughter, because I can't change that. I can tell you I'm sorry a million times, but I can't undo what's done."

He walked to her side and took her hands in his. "It's not that. I understood about your fear the day I saw Packard with a gun pointed at your head. I wish you would have trusted me enough to let me protect the two of you, but I understand why you felt you couldn't. The thing is, now I'm afraid."

She had trouble buying that, yet the shadowed depths of his dark eyes told her how serious he was.

"I'm afraid of losing you again, Trish, afraid that I'll build my world around you, and then some loose cannon—or at least the possibility of one—will show up and you'll just disappear from my life. That almost did me in at nineteen. I don't think I can handle it again."

"That's not going to happen, Langston. It took me years, I admit, but I'm finally past that."

"I guess I just need some kind of guarantee."

Her spirit plummeted, and her frustrations multiplied. "Life isn't a business deal, Langston. You have to trust me. If you can, I'll be there for you, loving you, for as long as I live. If you can't, then we don't have a chance of making it work between us."

Her words seared their way right to Langston's heart. She couldn't have made this any clearer. Trust her and have it all. Fail to trust her and lose her. There were times his stubbornness worked to his advantage. This wasn't one of them. Only a fool would let Trish walk away after all they'd been through.

He fell to one knee and took her hand in his. "I love you, Trish, with all my heart. I always have. Marry me and make my life complete."

"I was afraid you'd never ask."

"I'll take that as a yes."

And then she was in his arms. He kissed her as tears burned at the back of her eyelids, and the dreams of sixteen years finally came true.

* * * * *

Turn the page for a first look
at the next book in the
FOUR BROTHERS AT COLTS RUN CROSS
series,
Texas Gun Smoke *by Joanna Wayne.*
On sale in April 2009, only from
Mills & Boon® Intrigue.

Texas Gun Smoke

by

Joanna Wayne

A light rain started to fall, making the road that wound its way to Jack's Bluff Ranch dangerously slick. Not a safe night out for man nor beast. Most days Bart fell into the former category. He slowed his pickup truck and turned up the volume on his radio, singing along with Garth Brooks, though one of them was a bit off-key.

Bart stretched, then shed the necktie he'd loosed much earlier. He hadn't wanted to drive into Houston tonight, especially in this monkey suit. But his mother had refused to take no for an answer. Not that he didn't agree with her that philanthropy was important, or that her work in spearheading the drive to raise funding for the new children's wing at the hospital was a worthy task, but sipping champagne and making small talk with a gaggle of rich socialites wasn't his bag.

It still amazed him that his mother could dance from ranch life at Jack's Bluff to Houston society functions so effortlessly. The only dance Bart knew was the two-step, and that was the way he liked it.

His mom had opted to stay in town and spend the night with his brother Langston and his new family, leaving Bart to make the hour-plus drive home alone. Normally he wouldn't have minded, but tonight he could have used the company just to stay awake and alert. It had been a long day. Ranching was not a nine-to-five job.

He caught sight of a pair of bucks at the edge of the road in front of him. He slowed even more. You never knew when a deer would take a notion to run right in front of you.

The rain picked up. He turned on the defroster to clear the windshield, improving visibility only slightly, but he'd be home in less than ten minutes anyway.

He tried to stifle a yawn, then jerked to attention. What the hell? Two cars were speeding toward him, and the passing car was all but swapping paint with the other one.

A second later he saw sparks fly as the outside car sideswiped the other and sent it rocking and bouncing along the shoulder before the driver managed to get all four wheels back on the highway. If this was some teenage game of chicken, they were taking things way too far. Somebody was likely to get killed. Maybe him.

He slowed and took the shoulder as the cars collided again. This time the smaller one went flying off the road. It slid down an incline, rolled over, and came to a rocking, upside-down stop a few yards ahead of Bart. The lunatic driving the attacking car sped past him.

Bart screeched to a stop, grabbed a flashlight and jumped from his truck. He took off running toward the wrecked car. Its wheels were still spinning when he got to it.

He aimed a beam of illumination inside the car.

There was only one occupant, a woman who was draped over the steering wheel, upside down but still held in place by her seatbelt. Blood trickled across her left temple and matted in her blond hair. She lifted her head, shaded her eyes from the light and shrank from him.

The door was jammed, and he had to work with it for a few seconds to pry it open. "Are you okay?"

She didn't answer, but her face was a pasty white and her eyes were wide with fear.

"Take it easy. You're safe now."

"You tried to kill me."

"Not me, but someone did." He leaned in closer so that he could see the head wound. The cut didn't look particularly deep, but a nice little goose egg was forming. "What hurts?"

She stared at him, looking dazed, then touched her fingertips to the blood. "I must have hit my head."

"Probably against the side window when you went into the roll. For some reason your airbag didn't deploy."

"The light had gone off. I was going to get it checked."

A little late for that now. He pulled her against him while he unhooked the seat belt. He lifted her out of the car and stood her on the ground. She was lighter than a newborn calf and short, probably no more than five-two or –three. Thin, almost waiflike. But pretty. Movie-star looks.

She swayed and he put an arm around her shoulder for support. "My truck's over there." He pointed to where it was parked on the opposite side of the road. "Let's get you in it and out of the rain while we wait for an ambulance."

"No." Fear pummeled her voice. "No ambulance. I'll

be okay. I just…" She swayed again and might have lost her balance completely if he hadn't been supporting her. "I just need a minute for my head to clear. And I need my handbag."

"Right." He found it with its strap tangled in the brake and accelerator pedals. He worked it loose and handed it to her. She clasped it tightly in both hands.

Rain dripped from her hair and rolled down her face. He took the silk handkerchief from his breast pocket and wiped the water and blood away. "I'm not going to hurt you, but we need to get you out of the weather."

"Who are you?"

"Bart Collingsworth, and don't worry. I'm just a Good Samaritan who happened to be passing by."

She eyed him suspiciously, but let him lead her across the street. He helped her into the passenger seat and closed the door behind her.

He punched in 9-1-1 on his cell phone as he rounded the truck to the driver's side. Like it or not, he was calling for an ambulance and law enforcement. He was still giving the operator the information when he climbed behind the wheel.

"I know you said you didn't want an ambulance," he said, once he'd broken the connection, "but there's a small hospital in Colts Run Cross—not much more than a clinic with a few beds, but they'll call in a doctor to check you out. Better to be safe than sorry."

"I've already had more than enough of Colts Run Cross."

"I take it you're not from around here."

She stared out the front window into the darkness and rain. "Is anybody?"

"A few lucky souls. I live on a ranch a few miles down the road. Jack's Bluff. You just passed it."

She trembled and clasped her hands in front of her, nervously twisting her wedding band. "I didn't notice."

"Guess not with that last lunatic trying to run you off the road. What was that about?""

"I haven't a clue."

"But you must have had some kind of altercation with the driver."

"No. He came out of nowhere."

Either she was lying or this made no sense at all.

She leaned back and closed her eyes. She looked incredibly fragile, like a porcelain doll that had been left out in the rain.

"Are you sure you're okay?"

"I'm fine. I just don't feel like talking."

He left in at that until she finally shifted and opened her eyes, still looking straight ahead.

"You know if you really want to be a Good Samaritan," she said, "you could drive me into town and drop me off at a cheap motel. I can handle things from there."

"You were awful woozy back there. You'd be better off seeing a doctor, but you're welcome to use my phone if you want to call your husband."

"No thanks."

"I can call for someone to tow your car, or you can just wait and have the sheriff do it."

Finally, she turned to face him. "If you live on a ranch, why are you dressed like that?"

"It was tux night at the campfire. But I'm genuine. Got boots and spurs and everything."

"Then maybe you could get some of your cowboy

buddies to pull my car back to Jack's—whatever you said."

"Jack's Bluff."

"Right. Take the car there, and I'll come for it later."

"Your car's got four wheels straight up in the air. You need a tow truck for this job."

She shrugged. "I'm short on cash, and I don't have a credit card on me."

"Tell you what. I know a local mechanic with his own tow truck. I'll call Hank Turner and have him take the car to his garage. You can settle up with him later."

"Whatever."

"He'll want a name."

"Jaclyn."

Sirens sounded and Bart caught sight of flashing lights speeding toward them. The ambulance had made excellent time.

"Last name?" he asked.

She ignored the question.

He wasn't ready to give up yet. "If you're in some kind of trouble, you should level with me. Maybe I can help. I could at least follow the ambulance to the hospital and see that you're in good hands tonight."

"*In* trouble? I *am* trouble, cowboy. Thanks for the offer. But forget about the car. Forget about me, too. I'll be just fine." In spite of her assurances, a tear escaped and rolled down her right cheek.

Bart's insides kicked around like a stallion on a short rope. He had his doubts that anything she'd said tonight had been the truth. Well, except that she was trouble. Likely in trouble, as well. None of which was any of his business.

But he was wide-awake now, and the hospital wasn't but a few miles away. Besides, what red-blooded cowboy could resist trouble that came in a package that was five foot two and blonde?

Mills & Boon® Intrigue
brings you a sneak preview of…

Marie Ferrarella's A Doctor's Secret

*Dr Tania Pulaski vows never to get involved with
a patient. Then Jesse Steele enters her emergency
ward. Although he's strong and attractive, she
hesitates to take things to the next level…until
someone starts stalking her and she must trust
the one man who can help her.*

*Don't miss this thrilling new story available next
month in Mills & Boon® Intrigue.*

A Doctor's Secret by Marie Ferrarella

Tatania Pulaski loved being a doctor, or more accurately, loved being a resident. Tania was in her fourth year, that much closer to being able to hang up a shingle if she so desired. She loved everything about her duties, even the grosser aspects of it. Very little of what she dealt with at Patience Memorial Hospital fazed her.

Even so, she took nothing about her journey or her ultimate goal for granted. She, like her three older sisters and her one younger one, had paid her dues and was acutely aware of every inch of the long, hard, bumpy road it had taken to get here. She knew the sacrifices her parents had made and the contributions each of her older sisters had made. It was an unspoken rule: the older always helped the younger. It was just the way things were.

Although her heart was focused on becoming a spinal surgeon, there was no task Tania wasn't willing to do if the occasion came up. The only thing she didn't like were the rare moments that other doctors lived for.

A lull in the activity.

She didn't like lulls. Lulls caused her to think and, eventually, to remember. To remember no matter how hard she tried not to, no matter how often she forced herself to count her blessings first.

She had a great many of those and counting always took a while. She had a supportive family, parents and sisters who cared about her. Even her brother-in-law and the two men who, very shortly, were going to become part of the family were all nice guys.

On top of that, she was becoming what she'd always dreamed of being ever since Sasha, her oldest sister, had announced she was going to be a doctor. The revelation gladdened the heart of her father and, most of all, her mother.

All Tania had to do was to take in the scene that long-ago afternoon and that made up her mind for her. She was going to be a doctor. She, too, was going to save the world one patient at a time. The fact that Natalya and Kady followed in Sasha's footsteps only made her resolve that much stronger that she was going to be a doctor, too.

There'd only been one dark incident to cast a stain on her life, one in comparison to the multitude of blessings, and yet the shadow of that one stain managed to cast itself over everything, blackening her life like a bottle of ink marring a pristine white sheet.

One stain had caused all the happiness to slip into abeyance.

She tried, more for her family's sake than her own, to put it behind her. To forget. But forgetting for more than a few minutes at a time was next to impossible. The incident lived with her every day, shadowing her. The memory of it found her when she was at ease and assaulted her mind, making her remember. Making her suffer through it.

Especially in her dreams.

Trying to block it out of her mind was the reason why she'd eagerly volunteered to work in the emergency room every time the area was shorthanded. Ninety-nine times out of a hundred, the E.R. was crowded with patients, all seeking immediate help. The atmosphere was nothing short of frantic and hectic. And nothing made her happier than being there. She was forced to concentrate on procedures, on patients who needed her help.

And while she concentrated on that, the cold, hard

reality of what had happened to her that one horrible evening was pushed into the background.

For the time being.

This particular morning the bedlam that was called the E.R. seemed especially acute. A trauma bay was no sooner emptied than someone else was brought in to fill it. She'd been on duty for close to twelve hours, on her second "second wind" and had cleared over thirty-one cases before she stopped counting.

Tania felt dead on her feet and there were still several hours to go until her second shift was finally over.

Be careful what you wish for.

It wasn't an old Polish saying, like the ones her mother was so fond of quoting, but it certainly did fit the occasion.

She was just erasing the newest case she'd discharged, which meant she was up for the next patient, when another fourth-year resident, Debbie Dominguez, tugged on the sleeve of her lab coat.

When Tania glanced in her direction, the dark-haired woman pointed to the rear doors that just sprang open. The look in Debbie's eyes was envious.

"Boy, some people have all the luck." She referred to the fact that Tania was up for the patient being brought in by two ambulance attendants.

Strapped to the gurney was a tall, muscular man in what appeared to be a disheveled, gray suit. The patient's hair was several shades darker than her own blond hair and he didn't exactly look happy to be there.

Behind him were two more gurneys, one with an older, somber-dressed man and the second with a rather vocal patient. The latter had a police escort in addition to the two attendants bringing him in.

"I don't need a doctor," the man in the gray suit on the first gurney protested. "Really, all I need is just to get cleaned up."

The older man on the second gurney seemed noticeably concerned. "Please, young man, you need stitches. I know these things. I will take care of everything. The hospital, everything," he promised with zeal. "But you need to have medical attention."

The head ambulance attendant began rattling off the first man's vitals. Tania listened with one ear while giving the man on the first gurney a swift once-over. As far as patients went, they didn't usually come this exceptionally good-looking. While distancing herself, Tania could still see why Debbie had been so interested. Any more interested and the woman would have been salivating.

When her patient struggled to get off the gurney, Tania placed her hand on his shoulder.

"Listen to the man," she advised, nodding toward the second gurney. "He's right. Besides, if you put on another suit, you're just going to wind up getting blood on it unless I stitch you up."

Turning his head in her direction, Jesse's protest died in his throat. His eyes swept over her and he had to admit he did like what he saw.

"You're my doctor?"

Rounding the corner to the trauma bays, feeling as if she was at the head of a wagon train, Tania grinned in response to the appreciative note in the man's voice. "I'm your doctor."

Jesse settled back against the gurney. "I guess maybe I'll take those stitches."

"Good choice."

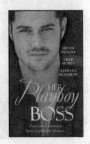

Passion. Power. Suspense.
It's time to fall under the spell
of Nora Roberts.

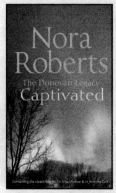

2nd January 2009

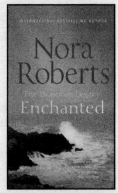

6th February 2009

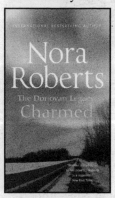

6th March 2009

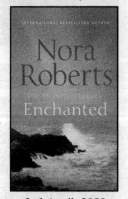

3rd April 2009

The Donovan Legacy
Four cousins. Four stories. One terrifying secret.

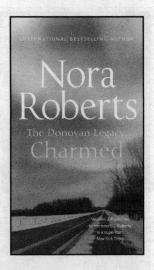

Secrets always find a place to hide…

When DEA agent Rodrigo Ramirez finds
undercover work at Gloryanne Barnes's nearby
farm, Gloryanne's sweet innocence is too much
temptation for him. Confused and bitter about
love, Rodrigo's not sure if his reckless offer of
marriage is just a means to completing his
mission – or something more.

But as Gloryanne's bittersweet miracle and
Rodrigo's double life collide, two people must
decide if there's a chance for the future they
both secretly desire.

Available 6th February 2009

FREE

4 BOOKS AND A SURPRISE GIFT!

We would like to take this opportunity to thank you for reading this Mills & Boon® book by offering you the chance to take FOUR more specially selected titles from the Intrigue series absolutely FREE! We're also making this offer to introduce you to the benefits of the Mills & Boon® Book Club™—

> ★ **FREE home delivery**
> ★ **FREE gifts and competitions**
> ★ **FREE monthly Newsletter**
> ★ **Books available before they're in the shops**
> ★ **Exclusive Mills & Boon Book Club offers**

Accepting these FREE books and gift places you under no obligation to buy; you may cancel at any time, even after receiving your free shipment. Simply complete your details below and return the entire page to the address below. You don't even need a stamp!

YES! Please send me 4 free Intrigue books and a surprise gift. I understand that unless you hear from me, I will receive 6 superb new titles every month for just £3.15 each, postage and packing free. I am under no obligation to purchase any books and may cancel my subscription at any time. The free books and gift will be mine to keep in any case.

I9ZEE

Ms/Mrs/Miss/Mr...Initials ....
BLOCK CAPITALS PLEASE

Surname ....

Address ....

....

....Postcode ....

Send this whole page to:

The Mills & Boon Book Club, FREEPOST CN81, Croydon, CR9 3WZ

Offer valid in UK only and is not available to current Mills & Boon Book Club subscribers to this series.
Overseas and Eire please write for details. We reserve the right to refuse an application and applicants must be aged 18 years or over. Only one application per household. Terms and prices subject to change without notice. Offer expires 30th April 2009. As a result of this application, you may receive offers from Harlequin Mills & Boon and other carefully selected companies. If you would prefer not to share in this opportunity please write to The Data Manager at PO Box 676, Richmond, TW9 1WU.

Mills & Boon® is a registered trademark owned by Harlequin Mills & Boon Limited.
The Mills & Boon® Book Club™ is being used as a trademark.